<u>Starting From Scratch</u> :

A True Love Story

By : Duane THE AUTHOR

Sometimes we have to regroup, pull ourselves together, and go back to the drawing board. There are also times when we lose everything and are forced to start over from scratch.

Some people must rebuild their lives from the ground up. It's called starting from the bottom. This is a difficult and time-consuming task that builds strength and resiliency.

Life is funny sometimes. Endless laughs and euphoric good times lead to memorable experiences that will be cherished for a lifetime. And then there are the countless heartbreaks and losses that cause even the strongest of human beings to break down.

So, when the levees break, the earthquakes, and plagues test one's faith; the survivors accept it as fate, and swim through tear-filled Lakes…searching and striving for something great.

— Duane The Author

Prologue

February 16, 2020

Even Sundays in Italy are considered sacred days. Since the beginning of time, the Sabbath day was to be one of rest, worship and resurgence. Abby found out about her Miracle on the Lord's day, and felt it was befitting to share the news with her family on a Sunday as well.

"Ok guys. I know you're wondering why I've been acting so weird lately —"

"Weird? You? Noooo, like *never!*" Jeanette-Mary teased her stepmom.

"Oh, hush Queen Jean. Let me finish," Abby responded with a smile.

"My bad, my bad. Go ahead mom."

"Thank you. Now as I was saying, there is something I want to share with you two," Abby looked from her husband to her step-daughter.

"Something I wasn't sure was true, but by the grace of God, it's been confirmed." Abby pulled a 9 x 12 manilla envelope from her purse and laid it on the tablecloth. She watched as the sun began to set over the beautiful architecture of Italy. Everyone at the table stared at the envelope in silence.

"Holy buckets! Will one of you open it please?" Abby exclaimed.

Jeanette-Mary didn't need to be told twice. She ripped opened the envelope like it was a college-acceptance letter. When she pulled out the black Thermal paper, she gasped in shock. "Noooo, way! Really?"

"Yes, *way!*" Abby beamed and nodded excitedly. The two women screamed and hugged lovingly. Noble reached over and picked up the paper. He looked at it, then looked at his wife. Tears formed in both of their eyes as her smile made him cheese from ear to ear.

"How can this be? I thought…" he trailed off and looked at the ultrasound in disbelief.

"I know right? We know what the doctors said. We've tried and thought for sure this wasn't possible. Even *I* was in denial. I took twelve pregnancy tests before I went to the doctor," Abby laughed. "I guess after eleven positive reads, I told myself all eleven can't be faulty. And the twelfth one made me go see my OBGYN. I'm twelve weeks pregnant. With *twins!*"

Suddenly, the long-haired waitress appeared with their drinks. Abby waited until she left until she commented on her distaste for Noble's drink.

"Ugh, I don't know how you can drink those Coronas."

Noble took a swig from the ice-cold long neck bottle. "Ahhh," he sighed satisfactorily. "Hey, I blame *you* for Americanizing me. I was never a beer guy —"

"Before Shawn. Don't go blaming me. *Shawn,* turned you onto your drink of choice," Abby reminded him.

"Yeah, yeah. Anyway, why did you not tell us this before?" Noble asked his wife.

"I'm really sorry hun. It was killing me to keep it from you guys, but I knew our vacation was coming up. I wanted to give y'all the good news in a special setting," she spoke in her country twang.

All three of them over-looked the restaurants terrace. Sitting on the second-floor balcony gave them a closer view to the rainbow-colored sky that cascaded over the lush green hills that seemed to go on for miles.

Everyone got lost in their thoughts while they processed Abby's news. Not one, but *two*, babies were on the way. Their worlds were about to be impacted in a major way.

"You should have told us about this asap mom. That was mean," Jeanette-Mary pouted.

"Yeah, well, now you know. So, quit giving me crap and just be excited that we're having −"

"A BABY!!!" They all shouted together.

****

January 12, 2007

Noblesse L' Ouverture, better known as "Noble," was walking in downtown Port-au-Prince, Haiti. The great people of Port-au-Prince called it "the loop," because pedestrians tended to walk around the area in laps (or loops). Tourists from all over the world looped the colorful storefronts that lined the busy streets. Tall stucco buildings were constantly buzzing with animation. There was something about the loops atmosphere that drew people in.

Although Noble knew his hometown better than the stats of his favorite athletes, he came across a small, boutique-like shop he could not recall seeing before. It was a bright red, shabby-looking, two-story structure. Pink letters were scrawled on the wooden shutters that flanked the narrow doorway. Something within his curious soul told him to go in, while another part of him said, *keep walking.*

"Welcome. Come in my son," a raspy voice came from somewhere. Noble cautiously entered the heavily incensed shop and looked around slowly. It was dark and smoky inside. Glow in the dark skulls and human teeth necklaces lined bookshelves, while tie-dye paintings adorned the walls.

"Please, be seated. I've been waiting for you," A female parted some beaded curtains and emerged from the back. She floated into Noble's presence wearing a long red dress with gold embroidery on the sleeves. Her long dreadlocked hair was thick and flecked with gray.

Noble looked around the small, clustered shop as his eyes began to adjust to the dark. When he spotted the human dolls and figurines, he knew immediately that he was in a place of Voodoo.

"Look, I… I don't partake in Voodooism," he stammered. "I didn't know what this place was. I can't remember seeing it before. I'll be going now. Good day." Noble turned to leave, but the woman grabbed his arm. He stopped in his tracks and stared at the exit sign. Stupefied by the woman's strong grip, he tried to pull away, but to no avail.

"Please, sit down," she said, holding his wrist in what felt like a death grip. He winced. "This is of very importance to you," she said, walking him to a small round table in the corner. He did as he was told, and she released his wrist. She sat opposite him, but she did not walk though. The way she moved, it was like a hovering, graceful, spectral-like apparition that gave Noble the chills.

"Noblesse, do you know why you've never seen my shop?"

"H-h-how did you know my name?" he stuttered.

The woman leaned forward. Her costume jewelry and beads jingled on the tablecloth. Blemish-free skin lined with "wise wrinkles" came to life with every word she spoke.

"Before today, this place never existed." Her dark green eyes sparkled like emeralds. Her lips didn't turn up, but she smiled at him… with her *eyes*.

"What are you talking about? And how did you know my name? What's going on here?"

Again, the eyes smiled. Her crows' feet curved upward like the wings of an Angel. She grabbed both of his hands and he jumped at how cold they were. Chills ran through his body and his *soul* shivered. It felt like he was being held by two ice blocks. *Wow, this lady is strong*, he thought to himself.

"Look into my eyes," her raspy voice demanded. When he did, images flashed in her pupils. Noble felt like he was watching a movie. The visuals were rapid bursts of things he could not make sense of.

"I am a woman of great knowing's. Now listen to me my son. Noblesse, you are a man of profound wisdom and integrity. You come from a legendary family, and only the most brilliant of strength flows through your blood. But three years from this very day, you and everyone you love, will be tested by the God's above. Haiti will suffer a terrible loss like never before. Mother nature will wreak havoc on us all. She will break our hearts, just to see if the people in the world have it in *their* hearts, to help rebuild the poorest country in the western hemisphere. You will experience significant pain unless you heed my advice and re-write history."

"Huh? What in the world are you saying lady? Re-write history?" Noble was bewildered.

"Take your family and go. Get out while you can. If not…"

"What? If I don't leave, what?"

The Angel wings rose again. Noble saw multiple coffins in her eyeballs, and he snatched his hands away quickly. The chair fell to the floor as he stood up and stumbled. He never took his eyes off the lady in red as he backed away slowly. Just as he reached the door, she smiled for the first time. Her yellow teeth lit up the room and her eyes turned black as coal. Noble opened the door and ran outside.

Sweat drizzled down his face like summer rain. A tug of war went on inside of his brain. On one hand, he thought the lady was crazy. She practiced something he did *not* believe in. All of that black magic stuff was a thing of the devil. But on the other hand, he saw visuals in her eyes that felt like Déjà Vu. He pondered his thoughts as he walked down the street. When he got to the corner, he looked back to where he just came from. There was no bright red building anywhere in site.

PART ONE

The Tragedy

Chapter 1

The Devastation

January 12, 2010

Noble was the head foreman of Haiti's main construction company. He oversaw ninety percent of the jobs throughout the island. They mostly built and maintained commercial buildings in Port-au-Prince and the surrounding cities like Léogâne, Carrefour, and Jacmel.

For the past few weeks, he had been adding on a structure to the Magnificent Church. It would eventually house a children's division for Bible studies and adolescent classes. It was an honor for him to work on the building his children would one day become students of God at.

Jeanette-Mary was his nine-year old beauty queen. She was a smart, vibrant girl, who liked fashion and glittery things. He nicknamed her "Queen Jean" because she acted like one every day of the week, thinking she was grown. He loved her enthusiasm and candor genuinely.

François, aka "Franky," was their middle child. Like most seven-year-olds, he was an avid video game lover.

Tai-Kembe was their shy, puppy dog eyes-having five-year old. All of them were children of God. Pure miracles from the man above. There was a time when Noble and his wife Genevieve thought they would never have kids.

He was 21 and she was 19 when they got married. For the first ten years of their marriage, they tried to conceive every day. Sometimes *multiple* times in a day. Just as their faith in procreation began to dim, along came Jeanette-Mary, then Franky. Tai was there last miracle.

Noble was blessed to have three beautiful children and a loving wife. He thanked God every day for the breath in their lungs. That's why he was determined to pour his heart and soul into the Church project. The new division would show a reflection of his love for children. Not just his own, but *all* of the youth.

The Magnificent Church job was a twenty-minute walk to the local school his kids attended, and his wife taught at. As was customary, he grabbed his lunchbox and said goodbye to his co-workers. When he headed northbound to pick up his family, an eerie feeling came over him. Someone in a red burqa walked towards him. All he could see were bloodshot eyes that matched their garment.

Thunder rumbled in the sky. He turned around, but the person who just walked past him was no longer there. Looking left and right, Noble spun around in circles. He was confused. There was no red dress in sight. *It's been a long day*, he thought as he shook his head and continued on.

Noble walked the busy streets of Port-au Prince greeting the locals he'd known for years. A lot of them were unemployed people and troubled teenagers who hung in the streets because they had nothing else to do. They were school dropouts with no regards for anything in life. The hopeless look that lived in their eyes was a deep pain that Noble felt in his own empathetic heart.

He tried to inspire as many kids as he could. There were cookouts in the park, football and basketball games at the playground, and hands on training at his construction sites. Noble made sure there were fun activities for all ages to participate in. But he wasn't their 24-hour guardian, and there was only so much that one man could do.

Close to 58% of Haiti is illiterate. Noble hated that well-known fact. That is why encouraging education was so important to him. But when the parents didn't care to learn how to read or write *themselves*, how could one coax their children to? It was a sad reality he hoped would be eliminated someday.

Noble looked up. The clouds vanished in the blink of an eye. A sky that was just a bright, brilliant blue, suddenly turned a dark, somber gray. A rigorous-like aura was in the atmosphere. Panhandlers, locals picking fresh fruit and vegetables from the street vendors, and teens smoking cigarettes, walked like Zombies as they stared at the sky with deplorable eyes.

The hairs on the back of Noble's neck stood erect and he froze in his tracks. Speed of light visions flashed before his eyes. A glow in the dark object and Angel wings were all he could make out. *What does that mean?* he thought to himself. A young kid riding his bicycle behind Noble had to suddenly swerve around him. In the process he lost control and fell off the bike.

"Are you ok?" Noble said, helping the young man get up.

"Yeah man, I guess so. Jeez, what cha stop like that for? I almost crashed into you!"

"Uh, I'm sorry about that. I think I just had a Déjà Vu moment," Noble remarked as he scratched his head.

"A what?" The kid asked puzzled.

"Never mind. Look, you really ride so close to people like that. Someone could get hurt," Noble said, standing the kids bike upright.

"Yeah, yeah. Gimme my bike sir. I gotta get home before this storm pours down." The multi-hair colored youth looked up at the sky, retrieved his bike, and pedaled down the road.

Noble dusted his hands off and rounded the corner. He was on a hill that had a straight-shot view of the school that was a few blocks ahead.

As always, he saw Franky and Jeanette-Mary standing on the third-floor balcony, waiting for him to arrive. Genevieve and Tai were cleaning up a classroom. Soon, all four of them would be on the balcony, waving and smiling as he made his way toward them. He'd make a funny face or do some kind of dance to entertain them. He loved to make his family smile. The infectious giggles of his kids were the highlights of his day.

He *heard* it, before he *felt* it. A loud, thunderous roar that came from deep within the earth's bowels. Noble slowed his pace and looked at his feet. In that split second all hell broke loose…

Mother nature needed the people of Haiti to look up at the sky, to distract them from the heart-wrenching destruction that tore up the ground below their feet. Sheets of lightning flashed across the sky like strobe lights in a nightclub. The black and gray marbling in the celestial regions was the setting of a horror flick. But this one was much more frightening.

The earth heaved in sickening undulations. It was a fierce viciousness that made Noble's insides vibrate. He lost his balance and fell to one knee. A telephone pole was shaken from its post and toppled over into the middle of the street.

"Daddy!" His children's screams reached his ears. He looked up and saw the terror in their eyes. They were clutching the handrails on the balcony, watching the chaos unfold. Genevieve was there now, rocking a frightened Tai-Kembe in her arms. Noble got up, hurdled the telephone pole, and saw doubles, as the streets went from a slight tremor, to a disconcertingly, raging shake!

People began to shout and run, but the earthquake was so intense, it made it difficult for them to get a few feet in distance before they stumbled or fell. Noblesse didn't have that problem though. His inner Superman came to life, and he ran with the sheer determination of a man possessed. He had to get his family to safety. All the determination in the world wouldn't stop mother nature from doing what she came to do.

The primary surface rupture produced visible fractures that slashed through the pavement. Concrete ripped apart like cloth linen. The earth's core *DEMANDED* to be fed, and the effects from the natural disaster did not disappoint. Houses, cars, people, and animals were all gorged into the huge chasms at a rapid pace. Horns blared, bricks shattered, and agonizing screams became the soundtrack that played during the 7.0 earthquake.

The school's rear structure was the first part to crumble. That caused the front of the building to catapult upwards like a seesaw and suspend itself in mid-air. Bodies rained from the sky like God was kicking people out of Heaven. Jeanette-Mary gripped the rail vehemently. In a silent plea for help, she stretched an arm out toward her father who was less than a block way.

"Almost there," he told himself. "Hold on, I'm coming!" Noble shouted at the top of his lungs. His heart raced uncontrollably as sweat drenched his body. Dust and debris filled the air courtesy of the brick and cement buildings being crushed like beer cans. Noble heard a loud explosion behind him as powerlines snapped like twigs and ignited propelling flames. Out of his peripheral, he saw the entire Heal Thy Neighbor Clinic disappear into the opened ground. His heart broke into a million pieces for the dozens of children and their families inside. Scores of innocent lives that sought medical help were now gone. Thousands of people would be in dire need of medical attention and emotional counseling once the catastrophe blew over.

A small Yorkshire terrier ran frantically ahead of Noble, a tiny ball of fur that tumbled down the chaotic street. Suddenly, a four-foot aperture divided the intersection. It looked like the dog jumped right into the gap instead of trying to make it to the other side. Maybe it was too frightened to no longer care. Maybe the small animal said, *screw it, we're all doomed anyway*," and willingly took the plunge.

Noble didn't feel that way though. The aperture the dog dived into stretched further and further apart. A green Volkswagen skidded down the steep hill, rolled end over end, and disappeared into the "abyss." Noble knew he had to hurry if he was going to make the jump. The incredulous opening got bigger by the second.

"Franky!" Genevieve screamed. Franky got whisked from the balcony as the railing broke. His thin frame swayed in the air like the Haitian flag on top of their school. He swung back and forth, fifty feet in the air, hanging onto the baluster for dear life. With the railing broke, Genevieve, Tai, and Jeanette-Mary could only look on with feverish hope.

Noble took a deep breath and channeled his inner Usain Bolt. "Hang tight! I'm coming!" He shouted and accelerated quickly. He ran and jumped with every ounce of his being. He landed with a loud thud on his stomach. His pelvis and legs dangled inside of the pit. If it weren't for the severity of the earthquake, he might have survived unharmed. But the monstrosity was so strong, so ferocious, it was like fighting a losing battle. Noble clawed at the concrete as it rose higher and higher. Blood covered his hands from the fingernails he left embedded in the ground. He desperately tried to pull himself out of the scalding chasm. It was the heat from the earth's core that charred his thighs and gave him a jolt of electricity.

He heard his arm snap like a feeble tree branch. "Arrrrrrgh!" Noble roared through gritted teeth. His right arm looked like a Cirque du Soleil contortionist. Using superhuman strength (and now one arm), he dragged the rest of his body out of the horrific, bottomless pit, that almost claimed his life. Thick clouds of dust filled his lungs, making him cough and wheeze. He crawled along the warm concrete, barely able to breathe.

Bracing himself with his good arm, he gathered up the strength to stand. The vibrating would not stop. A violent ripple tore through the streets and knocked him off his feet. A truck somersaulted down the road and landed on his legs, trapping him. He couldn't even feel the pain. It was the pain in his heart that immobilized him when he heard the loud crumbling noise. Through the truck's windows, Noble watched the school collapse before his very eyes. His wife and kids fell to their demise as he lay trapped beneath a vehicle.

The insufferable howl that he lamented could be heard as far as Cuba. It was a guttural, pain-filled cry that blanketed all of Haiti.

Noble heard footsteps approaching and looked to his right. The figure in red appeared next to him. All he could see were scaly feet that peeked out beneath the red garment. "I warned you, didn't I? I told you to get out, but you didn't listen," a female voice said before the feet walked away.

"Wait! Help me! Wait!" Noble shouted.

The wheels in his head began to turn. He thought back to what the Voodoo woman told him three years prior. Everything she said came true. *Was that her that just spoke to me?* He pondered.

He shook his head in disgust, *how could this be?* He thought to himself. He wished he had believed her. His angry fists pounded the pavement. *How could this be?!*

The sound of crumbling buildings, cars colliding, powerlines exploding, and people screaming, was a deafening collage of despair that penetrated every one of his senses.

Noble grunted as he tried to free himself. He reached this way, and stretched that way, but he was stuck. He gasped for breath while more smoke and dust clouds filled his lungs.

Tears and blood streaked his dirty face. It was a face that became a black canvas painted by pain and destruction.

He just lost his family. Seconds later, he lost consciousness.

Chapter 2

Abby

Abigail "Happy Abby" Winters walked around her favorite room in the house – the kitchen. She hummed a gospel hymn while she chopped vegetables for her Creole-style Gumbo. Some people thought she was crazy for cooking such massive meals. But they were nosey rubberneckers on the outside looking in. Although she lived alone, she wasn't cooking for just herself.

After she ate, she'd put a couple of servings up for lunch or a "snack." The rest of the food was put into Tupperware bowls and delivered to the homeless shelters and soup kitchens throughout the city. Abby loved to serve others. She believed it was her calling to do so.

After her world turned upside down in the blink of an eye, she learned to never take life for granted again. She realized there were a lot of people who got the short end of the stick in life, but if she could do anything about it, she would erase that feeling of dejectedness, one person at a time. Or at least one *smile* at a time.

Once Abby began volunteering her time and efforts at the local missions and shelters, the people she leant a helping hand to would often comment about how contagious her smile was. It didn't take long for her to acquire the nickname "Happy Abby." One could not help but to mimic her infectious beam whenever it lit up a room. Even the people who were miserable and hated life had to take a few seconds out of their depressed existence to smile whenever she did.

She hummed along to Michael Bublé's "Home" that played softly on the stereo as she filled her two-bedroom home with the appetizing smells of spicy gumbo. The delicious scents made her stomach do an anticipatory flip or two as it growled anxiously. Abby knew she should cut-back on the heavy-duty cooking (as advised by her Doctor), to prevent reaching "obese" levels. But she loved to cook, and she loved her full-figuredness even more. Abby was a true southern belle that embraced her curves whole-heartedly. She was in good health statistically, but by Hollywood standards, her "junk in the trunk" and wide hips wouldn't be landing her on the cover of Vogue any time soon.

That was fine by her, she didn't aspire to be something she was not. Abby was a curvy young woman that enjoyed running a few miles a couple of times a week and doing Pilates. She felt she'd be ok if she exercised. She did love her chocolate, but only as an occasional treat.

The combination of jalapeno peppers and onions made her nose run and eyes water. She walked to the living room and opened a window. The TV she passed was muted, but she could see the Breaking News report flashing on the screen. She grabbed the remote and turned the volume up. Stupefied, she sat on the edge of her sofa and watched in horror as pure chaos was broadcasted.

The ticker at the bottom of the screen read **7.0 Magnitude: Earthquake in Haiti**. A live report during the devastation gave the world an up close and personal view of one of the worst natural disasters in history. The camera shook in such disarray as it captured shot after shot of people running for their lives. Children cried and screamed, buildings collapsed, and greedy flames engulfed everything in its path.

Her eyes were glued to the tube. She always thought those reporters were insane to put their lives at risk in such deadly situations. When it came to their jobs, you could find them "in the eye of the storm." Hurricanes, tornadoes, earthquakes, tsunamis; they'd be right there, capturing all the footage. They might get blown away by thousand mile an hour winds, pounded by debris, or chased by billowing waves, but they were going to get their stories at all costs.

"Run for your life!" Abby shouted at the TV. "Don't try to capture other people's pain for your own journalistic agenda. Help someone for God's sake!" She remembered how many people were quick to shove cameras in her face during Hurricane Katrina and it angered her all over again. She hated re-living those life-altering events from 2005. Every time another natural disaster plastered the news, Abby was forced to endure those painful memories.

She was like many people who watched Haiti be decimated from the comfort of their own homes. Buildings crumbled into heaps of rubble. Roads buckled and parted like lovers whose relationship had lost its budding flames of passion. Rural communes were tumbled into utter ruin. Abby's heart broke into a million pieces as she witnessed the calamity. Some poor soul staggered down the street on fire. People ran right past him (or her), and the cameraman zoomed in on the burning person as if it was some sort of spectacle. You could feel the Haitian people's anguish as they suffered through an overwhelming ordeal.

Tears slid down Abby's cheeks as she looked up at the ceiling fan. "Please Lord. Have mercy on Haiti," she whispered. "Be with them during their darkest hour. We don't know why, but if this is what needed to happen, then let your will be done. And if there is anything you want me to do, please show me a sign… Amen."

She returned her attention to the television and saw various disaster relief organizations asking for help. In that moment, she knew what she had to do.

Through blurry eyes and trembling hands, she picked up the phone and dialed her traveling agent. "Book me on the next flight to Haiti," she said, and made further arrangements to fulfill her "calling."

Chapter 3

The Aftermath

There is always an end to a beginning. By the time Abby finished her prayer, the earthquake had subsided. Church bells clanged wildly, cables swayed, buildings danced, telephone poles leaned at all angles. Then… came silence.

The scene looked like a Christina Perri song. Scars that were clearly visible crisscrossed roads, highways, aqueducts, powerlines and pipelines. Secondary surface ruptures were the cracks caused by the intense shaking, and they were *everywhere*. Those ribbons of destruction were like spiderwebs etched into every square inch of Haitian soil.

Buildings were pulverized and completely decimated. Yet for all its destruction, the earthquake seemed to have struck in a surgical way. While one building was completely destroyed, the edifice next to it was left standing and unharmed. It was a puzzling sight to see. Most of the government structures were reduced to dust. The Health, Justice and Education

Departments were all gone. The Presidential Palace's dome had caved in, yet the Agriculture building had survived. The houses — mostly two-story, vulnerable wooden structures crowned with heavy roof tiles — had not only been smashed, but they were completely shredded! Once sturdy material was rendered into splintered beams. Raveled and torn fragments of boards were jumbled together and strewn in every direction.

The capital itself was on fire. Emotionally and *literally*. Businesses and homes were saturated in flames due to exploded powerlines and combustible materials. Families fought to save their loved ones from burning buildings, only to become incinerated victims themselves. Clouds of black smoke hovered in the air as the streets became the devil's playground.

Those who weren't physically harmed used their emotional melancholy as an excuse to rebel. Commotion, disorder, and violence erupted into riots fueled by desperation and despair. People began looting stores and snatched any salvageable merchandise they could carry. Food, clothing, electronics, toiletries and weapons were among the many confiscated items being carried into the streets.

Two women fought over a case of bottled water. One man kicked a boy in his back and wrestled packages of meat from his grasp. A group of teens filled garbage bags full of chips and candy from a smoldering convenience store. There were even scavengers going through the pockets of lifeless bodies that littered the pavement. Jewelry, cash, cellphones, even *shoes*, were removed from the countless victims that perished in the travesty.

Ghastly cries were heard ubiquitously, while survivors searched for family and friends. Pairs of legs futilely stuck out from underneath disintegrated buildings. An eight-year-old girl with a massive head wound staggered from a garage. She dripped blood on a teddy bear that she clutched to her diminutive frame. A husband carried his fatally injured wife on his back. Even with a sprained ankle and a several mile trek to the general hospital; it was perseverance over pain for that brave man.

Pandemonium was rampant. The careless added to the body count by displaying senseless acts of violence. Machine gun fire rang out as the streets of Haiti became a battle zone. It was every man, woman, and child for themself.

But for all the onslaught, help began to show up in droves. Heroic doctors, nurses, and volunteers gathered as many medical supplies as they could and dispensed them to the most tragic scenes. Empathetic rescuers ventured out into the street to save lives, while a quarter of the other certified aids stayed behind to attend to the wounded being carried into the few remaining care facilities.

Support from all over the world was on its way. In the meantime, the good people of Haiti banded together and demonstrated why L' Union Fait La Force ("Unity is our strength") was their personal motto.

Men were running through the streets carrying stretchers over their heads. Many of them were transporting amputees. There were so many people with broken limbs and horrendous injuries.

One man was pinned by his arm inside a burning building. It collapsed just as he was about to escape. He was rescued by civilians that sawed his arm off while they beat at the flames with their flannel jackets.

This was a natural disaster of catastrophic nature. Burn victims, amputees, people with abrasions from the concrete and fallen objects were *everywhere*. Rivers of tears and gallons of blood were shed. It was a painful sight for anyone to see.

Meanwhile, Noble was one of the first people delivered to the hospital. A young man by the name of Ares was riding by on his Moped when he saw Noble lying unconscious in the middle of the street.

Ares knew Noble all his life. He respected and honored the man in a father-figure like way, for demonstrating his love to lost souls and troubled youth such as himself.

With the help of a few people in the vicinity, Ares was able to get Noble onto the Moped. Transporting the 6'3" 250-pound Noblesse was a bit of a task for the young man, so two other men stood on both sides of the bike and held Noble up while

Ares steered. They jog-walked to keep pace with the motorbike, but they got to their destination.

Nurses frantically attended to Noble immediately. Everyone in the community knew him as a great, upstanding man, so there was genuine concern.

Kiara (an RN and one of Genevieve's closest friends), saw Noble being dragged in. She stifled a scream and helped load him onto a gurney. His vital signs were checked, and he was declared comatose. Ares quickly swiped a tear off his cheek as he left the hospital with an inner rage boiling inside of his soul. He looked up at the Heavens and questioned the higher power he was beginning to doubt.

Meanwhile, Port-au-Prince was immersed in pure chaos. People were dragging their deceased loved ones from the rubble and laying them in the streets; only to be trampled on by looters and frightened Haitians running from the violence. Fires seemed to burn forever because Haiti was such a dry, brittle country.

Helicopters and airplanes began to arrive from all over the world with vast amounts of food, water, and medical supplies just hours after the devastation. Besides Port-au-Prince, other cities in the southeastern region of the country had been devastated as well. The magnitude was a record setting 7.0 that ripped through thousands of miles of once solid earth.

Sadly, before Rigor mortis in the deceased bodies could set-in, authoritative powers behind the scenes were already plotting the unthinkable.

Chapter 4

Éminence Grise

In a dark, shabby warehouse, stood a dozen men with AK-47's strapped to their backs.

"The time to strike is now! Our country is in shambles. The people are vulnerable, and our government is weak. They're too passive," a man named Slice said. "You see how it is out there. It's every man for himself. There are renegades every-where you look! I will have no such disorder in my organization. With my resources and leadership, we can recruit and train those radicals and become the most revolutionized carte blanche this country has ever seen!"

Cheers erupted as the men high-fived and fist-bumped each other. Slice (who got his nickname from the gruesome scars on his face), lit a joint. The cherry on his ganja cigarette glowed brightly as he inhaled. Tendrils of smoke wafted from his nostrils while he "rallied his troops."

"There will be millions of dollars pouring in from all over the world, and we will be the ones who regulate it. Haiti is ours!" Slice exclaimed.

"Haiti is ours!" the men repeated, raising their fists and guns in the air.

"I would not be a true leader if I did not warn you of the consequences." Slice said. "There will be people who won't submit easily. You will be putting your life on the line for this cause. *OUR* cause. So, if you aren't prepared to die…this regime is not for you. My soldiers are true warriors."

"Warriors!" the men shouted in unison.

"A legion of riders and troops on a mission. A brigade to be reckoned with!" Slice took another drag from his joint. He walked around the circle of men patting each one on his back.

"There is power in numbers. You all are my lieutenants, and I trust you to carry out this mission precisely. We will continue to grow by the day because the people are going to need someone to believe in. They need someone to turn to during these dark times. And those who *won't* roll with us? Well, they will get crushed!

Men, I can promise you great wealth, big homes, luxury cars, more ganja than you can smoke, and *lots* of beautiful women!"

"Women!" This revved the men up greatly.

"This is your final chance to bow out. Once this train is in motion, there will be no getting off. Death is the only way out. Anyone here want out?" Slice blew rings of smoke while the room grew silent. The smoke he exhaled cast an eerie light on his facial scars. It made him look even *more* menacing than he already did. When no one spoke up, he continued.

"Alright then. Bête Noire is official. Bête Noire!"

"Bête Noire!" The men shouted ecstatically and celebrated together.

****

Abby looked out the window of the plane arriving in Haiti. She admired how peaceful it looked. There were tall mountains, pretty blue water, and the greenest trees she'd ever seen. The magnificent view from the sky took her breath away.

As the plane grew closer to landing, she saw those objects from afar did not appear to be so peaceful after all. Fires still burned quietly in some places. Black smoke filled the air like polluted chimneys, and it floated through every block in Port-au-Prince.

Her heart ached as the empathy she felt for those she would soon encounter immersed her.

Get yourself together Ab, she told herself. She knew she couldn't expect *them* to be strong if she looked shattered herself. She closed her eyes and took a deep breath. Her heavy bosom rose and fell as she gathered her composure and thought positive things. When she opened her eyes again, she was at the airport.

It was crawling with an earnest military presence. UN soldiers patrolled the terminals trying to calm the evacuees desperate to escape. The US military was also in full force, coordinating operations for the dozens of planes and choppers coming in and out of Haiti.

Abby walked through the airport carrying her small bag. She passed Helicopters, Aircrafts, and Armored vehicles that filled the staging areas. Supplies were being distributed at an alarming rate. Children with serious wounds and lacerations wept in the arms of their mothers. The men, who were understandably frustrated and stressed out, could be heard aggressively shouting in French.

"Ennui" and "A bientôt" was said over and over by hundreds of Haitians. Abby saw the registration booth to the relief effort organization she would be working for in the terminal.

A young pixie-blonde woman manning the booth greeted her with a smile. "Hi, how may I help you?"

"I would like to sign up and lend my time in whatever services you may need," Abby said.

"Oh, ok. That's great. We usually require a three-month minimum commitment. However, we will gladly accept any time you can sacrifice."

"Um, I can do the three-months," Abby replied.

"Great! Will you fill out these forms so we can get you set-up with a team?" Pixie-blonde asked. Abby nodded and accepted the paperwork. "You will be out in the field helping to restore the community, so you won't be needing many possessions."

"Yes, I know how it is. I only brought this," Abby said, holding up her teal duffle bag.

"Good. So, I take it you've volunteered before?"

"Yes, I have. I am from New Orleans. After Hurricane Katrina changed my life, I've been doing whatever I can do to help others who've suffered from these unfortunate disasters."

The young blonde woman grabbed Abby's hand and held it in her palms. "God bless you. It's people like you who help make our organization what it is. Thank you so much for your generosity."

Abby nodded and sat down. She filled out the necessary paperwork and returned it to the young woman. Once she was done, she was introduced to her "team."

They were a diverse group of volunteers who would stick together as they contributed to the relief efforts of the organization. There was Hailey, a 25-year-old data entry specialist from Bryan, Texas.

Eric was a 34-year-old struggling actor from Los Angeles.

Nicole, 42, was a social worker from Augusta, Maine.

Tim, the youngest of the bunch, was fresh out of High school. He was a vibrant young man from Milwaukee, Wisconsin.

And the last of the crew was BJ, a personal trainer from Atlanta, Georgia. He just turned 30 the day Haiti was struck by the earthquake. The six of them quickly got acquainted as they gave Abby the rundown on their agenda.

"First and foremost, we need to deliver the medical supplies to all of the functioning hospitals and makeshift wards," Eric said, as he went over the plan. "Most of the streets are cluttered with debris and dead bodies, so our walks transporting this stuff won't be easy." Everyone nodded knowing the difficult task ahead of them.

"I've been given a map. There are seven main hospitals we need to cater to first. A lot of the roads are blocked because of the damage. Getting to the heavily devastated areas is going to be hard. Don't get frustrated, and please be safe. A lot of endangered people are still trapped and barricaded in places that they can't get out of, but we will do our best to help them. God willing…" Eric trailed off.

Everyone bowed their heads in a moment of silence as each team member got lost in their own thoughts. Abby's lower lip trembled as her emotional state overwhelmed her. *Be strong,* she told herself. She had to turn the water works off before the dam behind her eyes broke through.

"Let's all join hands," Hailey said. "Dear Lord, please give us all the strength and courage to fulfill *YOUR* mission. Allow us to rescue and save survivors from this horrible tragedy. A lot of people out there have lost everything! Please give us the right tools to help aid those in dire need. Keep us safe as the six of us embark on this journey of restoration, healing, and relief. We know better than to question your actions. Allow us to act in a manner pleasing to *you*, for everything happens for a reason. Even miracles can blossom out of mayhem. In Jesus' name we pray… Amen."

"Amen," everyone concluded. As they walked out of the Airport, Abby looked at the families packed in like sardines. They would all have to start from scratch.

****

Slice fulfilled his promise and took to the streets rallying the crooks, radicals, thugs and bad boy wanna-be's. "Roll with us or get crushed!" was the motto that could be heard on every block in Port-au-Prince as Bête Noire fired semi-automatic weapons in the air on dirt bikes and four-wheelers, (the only vehicles sleek and efficient enough to maneuver through the wreckage).

A young man by the name of Ares and his clique of teenage boys watched from dark alleys and barely standing rooftops as Slice and his Regime tore through Haiti with complete subversion.

"They're strong, but they have no discipline," Ares told his clique. "We're gonna have to put a stop to Slice before he ruins what is left of our country. He's a cockroach!" Ares spat over the ledge of the rooftop as if he had a bad taste in his mouth. "He's going to wreak havoc and mess a lot of things up if we don't step in." A chorus of mhm's and you're right, were concurred.

"Bête Noire is going down! We're young goon militants. YGM for life!" Ares shouted.

"YGM for life!" They all responded enthusiastically and fist-bumped each other.

"We may be young, but we're proud Haitians who will fight for the people and restore our country. We'll see who the real éminence grise is," Ares said, stroking his babyface chin.

Chapter 5

A Helping Hand

Abby was drenched in sweat as she hauled box after box into the General Hospital. It was a hot, muggy day, and the air was even more suffocating because of all the fire and smoke still lingering in the air.

Her team was very friendly and easy to get along with. They all worked equally as hard. They had dozens of boxes of medical supplies to distribute, but with the six of them working together, their efforts were more effective and timesaving.

Abby was introduced to Kiara, an RN who frantically ran to and fro, trying to care for the numerous patients that were brought in.

"Kiara, where would you like this penicillin?" Abby asked.

"Come with me," Kiara said, and walked down a long corridor. "You can put them in that room," she pointed to the last door on the right-hand side.

Abby entered the small room the size of a jail cell. A lone man occupied the intimate room hooked up to a machine. There seemed to be tubes running in and out of every part of his body. Abby sat the box down on the floor and pushed it against the wall. Her eyes were transfixed on the hulking figure that took up the entire bed.

His eyes were closed, and he looked so peaceful. His smooth ebony skin was a bit ashen, but it still shone. Even with all the cuts and abrasions covering him, Abby still considered him to be a very handsome man. His cheekbones and strong jawline complimented his chiseled features. His full, plum-colored lips were dry. Abby wanted to reach out and moisten them by nourishing him with a bottle of water. But she refrained. Unconsciously, she licked her lips.

Kiara came into the room. "Abby, are you ok?"

"Huh? Oh, yeah. I just…"

Kiara sighed loudly. "Such a tragedy isn't it? He was such a great man."

"Who is he?" Abby inquired, unable to stop gazing at the commanding presence before her.

"His name is Noblesse L 'Ouverture. But we all call him Noble. His wife Genevieve is my best friend..." Kiara began to tear up and Abby put an arm around her.

"It's ok Kiara. Everything will be alright."

"No, it won't! I got word that the school she worked at collapsed. And supposedly, there are no survivors."

"Oh my God!" Abby shrieked in horror, throwing her hands to her mouth.

"Yeah. Noble was found a block away from the school. He usually picks his wife and three kids up after work every day."

"So, what happened to him?" Abby asked, walking up to his bed to observe the sleeping Giant.

"I'm not sure exactly," Kiara said, joining Abby by Noble's bedside. She patted his hand gently. "He's been in a coma since he arrived four days ago. His right arm is broken. He also has a broken leg, fractured pelvis, and severe head trauma. He's lost a lot of blood. Dr. Moore said his survival is probable, but it will be difficult pulling through because of the fluid in his lungs. We are all hoping and praying for the best though. This man is truly one of Haiti's finest."

For the second time, Abby put her arm around the young woman. This time Kiara rested her head on Abby's shoulder and sighed. They both looked down at Noble peacefully.

"It'll work out. Angels are watching over him," Abby said, as she consolingly stroked Kiara's arm.

"Let's hope so. This is a great man. And if he's lost his family? I just..." the sobs burst through and racked Kiara's petite body like a seizure. Abby held her and let the young nurse bawl her eyes out until there was nothing else left inside.

****

Caring people from all walks of life sent help to Haiti. The empathetic reacted to the tragedy immediately. Money, food, and clothing were donated in bulk. Merchants dispatched truckloads of food and medical supplies by the tons.

And the volunteers?

People from all over the world; black, white, red and brown, donated their time and energy to the natural disaster crisis. Thousands of volunteers flew into Haiti daily and leant their blood, sweat, and tears to dozens of relief organizations.

Many people walked along the streets with backpacks and respirator masks. Some wore bandanas tied over their mouths. The baffling matter wasn't that they looked like gangbangers, but the care-free manner people strolled along the crowded streets, like a devastating freak of nature hadn't just tore their country in half. Behind everyone's "mask," there was a story. But just looking on the outside, it was hard to determine who was impacted.

Blankets, sheets and tarps were pitched up everywhere. They served as living quarters for the displaced victims. These heavily populated areas were known as "Tent City."

The once immaculate Presidential Palace had become a heaping pile of bricks in its most pancake-like manner. Directly across the street was probably one of the biggest Tent cities in Port-au-Prince. As if the people were trying to send their President a message.

The immense poverty that Haiti had been plagued with for decades, was a slow deterioration that sped up rapidly due to the earthquake. This culminated their problems into a dreadful storm.

Volunteers helped survivors poke through debris and rubble for their family-heirlooms and other belongings. Many found out that scavengers had pillaged their wrecked homes for anything salvageable. Priceless valuables were confiscated and bartered for food and other essentials.

There were hundreds of victims trapped under their own homes or deceased from suffocation. Many survivors wouldn't find out for quite some time where their loved one's bodies were. That's why a particular organization focused their efforts on hauling bodies from the wreckage and providing proper burials for the deceased if the family couldn't. Because of the grotesque conditions of the corpses, only those with strong stomachs were called to assist with that mission.

There was an overwhelming responsibility to bury the dead. A lot of survivors felt they cheated death and wanted to send their loved ones and associates out in the most respectable manner. People were transporting coffins on the roof of their cars and carrying caskets on foot.

For every half dozen "proper burials," twenty to thirty "throwaways" were wrapped in sheets and thrown in parking lots, or on the side of the street like litter. Toes peaked from beneath the sheets that occupied parks, cluttered roads, and parking lots with makeshift graves.

The looting had subsided once everything that could be taken was gone. Men with machine guns walked the streets with pain and anger in their hearts. None of this deterred the volunteers that entered the most dangerous areas.

When the radicals saw that their intimidation tactics did not work on the aides, they left them alone and allowed them to do their job.

Hospitals and clinics became so full, they had to set up hospices outside of the medical facilities. Tents with makeshift beds and stretchers held the gravely wounded and the half-dead. Volunteers got crash-courses from nurses and doctors that administered various medical techniques.

Abby tended to a little girl's head wound as she lightly dabbed peroxide on her wound. The child winced and Abby rocked her in her arms.

"What's your name?" Abby asked.

She looked up with her big, brown, puppy dog eyes and replied, "Fleur."

"Fleur? Ohh, that's such a pretty name."

"Mommy said it means Flower!"

"Really? That's awesome." Abby replied.

"Yup. What's your name?" Fleur asked.

"Happy Abby," she responded with her million-watt smile. Abby continued attending to the girl's wound while chatting her up. A gauze was secured, then she wrapped a bandage around her head. Fleur gave Abby a big hug once she was done. Two UN Soldiers came to escort Fleur back to the Tent city where her family was trying to rebuild their lives at.

Fleur looked back and waved. "Bye-bye happy Abby. Thank you."

"You're welcome sweetie. Bye-bye." Abby's eyes teared up as she watched the innocent girl walk out of her life and into a humanity that would not recover for years to come.

✱✱✱✱

The days flew by. Abby and her crew were one of the most dedicated teams in the field, often forgoing sleep in order to serve. They helped build shelters and feed hundreds of families. They nursed victims back to health and provided emotional and spiritual support for those who felt helpless. They even held prayer vigils in the most cataclysmic areas.

One night they took a much-needed break and went for a swim in the sea. Afterwards, they set up a bonfire and loosened up by having some drinks.

"Ahh, I really needed this," Eric said, taking a swig from a beer bottle.

"Yeah. We've really been going hard for like what, a week now?" Tim commented.

"Eleven days," Nicole corrected.

"Eleven? Holy buckets! It only seems like four or five to me," Abby replied.

"You're right Abbs, it feels like I just got here yesterday," BJ said.

"I know right?" Hailey said holding her hands over the fire.

"I feel so bad for these people. They have to start their lives over from scratch," BJ said.

"Yeah, I know what that feels like," Abby whispered. The rest of their chatter went unheard as Abby reflected on the pain and grief that she experienced during Hurricane Katrina.

Water, vehicles, bodies and debris floated for miles, as far as the eyes could see. Abby used her car door as a raft, and floated through the city, watching the chaos unfold. She held her stomach and looked up at the gray sky.

Please Lord, spare my child. Save us from your wrath, she prayed. Rain poured down on her face and the currents pushed her along as she held on for dear life.

Boats full of people zoomed past her with no regards. She saw people on rooftops holding signs that read SAVE ME and HELP. She couldn't do anything because she needed saving herself. She didn't remember blacking out, but when she came to, her world had changed for the worse.

Chapter 6

Emotions Run High

There seemed to be only two emotions flowing through Haiti… Pain, and love. There was no, in between. When Noble awoke, he was weak and extremely thirsty. His words came out in mere "croaks."

Kiara was going from patient to patient, running around like a chicken with her head cut off. During her rounds, she passed Noble's room and saw him moving around. She ran into the room and told him to relax and calm down. He was trying to tell her something, but she couldn't understand his mumblings. Frustrated, he lifted his arm and tilted his hand back a couple of times.

"Oh, eau potable. Of course, of course! Hold on, I'll be right back," Kiara said and dashed to get him some water.

After hydrating him, Kiara fed him a small meal and tried to help him garner his strength.

A couple of days went by and his recuperation was one of the fastest any medical staff had ever seen. His resiliency to heal and get out into the field was tenacious. That and the fact everyone in the hospital was mum about his family's whereabouts. He didn't know where his family was, but he needed to know that his wife and children were ok.

"So, you don't remember anything from that day?" Dr. Moore asked Noble.

Noble walked next to the doctor on crutches. Despite a broken leg and fractured pelvis, Noble walked the halls on his crutches to strengthen his mobility.

"No, I'm sorry. I don't." Noble replied.

"It's alright. You did suffer some head trauma. I'm surprised you even remember your *name,* after the condition you were found in. We had to do a blood transfusion because you lost a considerable amount of blood.

You being in a coma for two weeks was a nightmare for all of us here. You just don't know how important you are to us Noble," Dr. Moore confessed as they walked.

Noble smiled weakly as his crutches click clacked down the narrow hallway. "Thank you, Doctor. My *family* is the most important thing to me, and I need to know where they are."

Dr. Moore patted his back encouragingly. "Noble, there is so much rubble that people are still trapped under buildings. As far as the school, it collapsed in so many ways, they are still digging it up. The fatalities will be numerous, I'm sorry."

Noble nodded his head somberly. He knew the inevitable, he just wanted to find their bodies so he could bury them on the L' Ouverture plot that he owned.

"Noble, Haiti is going to need you when you get back to full strength. I hate to pressure you, but your leadership and integrity is the only thing to combat the perils of evil."

Noble paused. "What do you mean?"

Dr. Moore sighed heavily and patted Noble's back. "Get better first, then we'll talk. Ok?"

"What about my family? Will you let me know if they are found?" Noble asked.

The Doctor looked at the floor. "Noble, I… I'll keep you posted," he said and walked away.

Noble could tell something was wrong by the demeanor of Dr. Moore. The only time a Haitian man doesn't look another Haitian man in the eye, is when he's lying or hiding something.

I've got to get out of here, Noble thought to himself. He had too many questions and not enough answers.

****

Refugees patiently queued up for food at one of the biggest Tent cities in Haiti. Hundreds of thousands of meals were being served daily from the food organizations that fed the earthquake victims. Selfish bully's returned for seconds and thirds, bogarting their way in line, causing a shortage to those who hadn't even gotten *one* meal yet.

Emotions ran high. Seditious radicals worked hard to impugn the Haitian government. Slice and his Regime reigned supreme. Their debauchery of the vulnerable ardently contributed to his cause. Slice saw his vision come into fruition and his ego was multiplied. Hurt and lost souls whose faith was shattered by a 7.0 magnitude, became conducive to Bête Noire's subversion.

"Roll with us or get crushed!" was the inescapable chant not only suffusing Haiti's streets, but Carrefour, Leogâne, and Jacmel had it too. Slice was *everywhere*.

With so much rubble, it made it difficult for adequate aid to enter the small neighboring cities that got hit hard. Those cities were only accessible by narrow roads. Bête Noire's four-wheelers and dirt bikes thrived off those real-life courses. They used those small roads to wreak havoc and recruit lost souls who needed something to believe in.

People were so angry from lack of assistance, death of loved ones, the loss of their whole lives, and wondering why God allowed such calamity, that Slice's promises penetrated a lot of those susceptible beings. When he ranted about taking Haiti back and giving it to the people, it motivated and inspired them.

The media continued to pump out Live footage, broadcasting Haiti's pain on all the major networks. CNN in particular was essential in getting the people of the world to donate, donate, donate.

Images of babies piled up, three or four people sleeping in the trunk of a car, and limb-less citizens wandering the streets, were horrifying depictions that affected everyone. $300 could purchase a prosthetic limb for an amputee victim. There were so many amputees broadcasted on the news, viewers helped as much as they could.

Bodies continued to be discovered daily as the wreckage was cleared. A few miracle survivors were found under collapsed buildings. Those were marveling signs of hope for the desperate families that had not yet located their loved ones.

Emotions ran high. Pain, love, fear, hostility, optimism, and supplication floated in the atmosphere. Noble felt all of the above flowing through his veins.

He snuck out of the Hospital one night on a mission to seek answers. It was his first time outside, and his first destination was his home. What once was a peaceful, happy house, looked like a pile of dirt.

A telephone pole fell on the roof and set his *un hotel* (nobleman's house), on fire. It was like that with the other houses on the block too. They had all crumbled and burned to the ground. Noble was *n 'avoir ni feu ni lieu* (to have neither house nor home).

He picked through the burnt wreckage prudently. The picture frames that held his family's photos were charred. The pictures may have disintegrated, but he knew the visuals that once occupied every frame…

Tai-Kembe at his third birthday party, grabbing a piece of cake with his eager hands.

Franky and Jeanette Mary sticking their tongues out at a picnic.

Franky making bunny ears behind Tai's head last Christmas.

Noble and Genevieve kissing on their wedding day.

Noble limped over to a pile of soot and sat down. Tears fell onto the empty picture frames that filled his lap. The memories of those missing pictures came flooding back.

"It didn't happen here Noble," a voice said behind him. He jumped in surprise.

"Kiara, how did —"

"I know you were here? A woman's intuition," Kiara said and smiled. She stepped over metal pipes and splintered boards to get next to Noble. He looked up at her and attempted to stand. "Ah-ah. Don't get up. You snuck out of the hospital looking for answers. I have some things to tell you, and you're gonna want to sit for this," she looked around and sighed.

"When I came to check on you and saw that you were M.I.A. I knew you'd be here. You've been asking about Gen and the kids from the time you came out of your coma. We all agreed you should be brought back to strength before…" Kiara trailed off as she fought back tears.

"Before what Kiara? What is going on?"

"I went to the spot where Ares found you lying unconscious."

"Ares found me?"

"Yes. If he hadn't gotten to you when he had, you would have never made it. He brought you in and left quickly. I had to hunt him down to find out what he knew about that day. You were found a block away from the school. We think you were on your way to get them when your accident occurred. You were pinned under a pick-up truck. Who knows what all you went through that day, but God was with you Noble. Gen and the kids didn't make it though. I'm sorry to tell you… there were no survivors at the school. Witnesses have come forth and said they saw them go down when the school collap −"

"Stop! Just stop! It can't be. So, you're telling me my family is dead? Gone?"

"I don't know what to say. Soldiers are still clearing the wreckage, but it will be a while before all of the remains will be confirmed," Kiara choked up and began to cry. "I… I'm so sorry Noble."

He rocked upright, grabbed his crutches, and exerted to stand. Noble hugged Kiara tightly. His tears fell in her hair while hers dampened his shirt. He knew how much Genevieve meant to Kiara. Despite their age difference, they had been the best of friends ever since Kiara helped deliver Franky. The kids all knew her as "Aunt Ki-Ki."

Noble looked up and down his block. It looked like every other street he encountered when he left the hospital. A big vestige; like the love in Haitians hearts.

It was going to take a lot of rebuilding to salvage his country. Something in his gut told him he'd be summoned to play a major role in the restoration. When Dr. Moore's eyes told him that his integrity would be needed to fight the perils of evil, the look in his eyes bothered Noble. Everyone wanted him to do something for them, but all he wanted was his family. Noble would not rest until he found them. Dead or alive, he needed closure for his own heart.

Chapter 7

Noblesse Oblige

The first time he saw her, the sun was shining brightly. Abby was carrying a baby on each hip. Each infant was swaddled in bandages while she emerged from the hospice with them. She said something to each child in her arms and smiled. It was her smile that hypnotized him.

Her teeth glowed as if her mouth was a halo. Her supple pink lips turned upwards and caused the deepest dimples he'd ever seen, form in her cheeks. The sun made her white teeth bling like diamonds. Noble was short of breath watching her.

"Noble, you alright?" Ares walked up and asked.

"Ares? What are you doing here?" Noble said, not expecting to see the young man.

"A little bit of nothing," Ares replied. "Now, answer *my* question Noble."

"What's that?"

"I asked if you were alright. You looked like… I don't know. Like you were dizzy or saw a ghost or something."

Red visuals flashed before Noble's eyes and he quickly shook them away. "Um, I'm fine."

"You sure?" Ares asked with a raised eyebrow.

"Yes, I'm sure. Hey, I heard you were the one that saved me. I want to thank you –"

"Ahh, no need. You've done so much for me and everyone else Noble. When I saw you laying there, I was praying it wasn't too late."

Noble looked at the young man. He remembered when Ares was knee-high, getting into all sorts of mischief. His parents Zeus and Hera had their own domestic issues that contributed to the toxic environment of Ares' broken home.

When Noble started the local football and basketball games, Ares was one of the first kids to participate. It worked for a while, but the streets were vying for his attention and captured his interest. Noble knew he was only one man and could only do so much. He wished he could parent every kid in Haiti and raise them with love and adoration. Those were the key ingredients needed to raise Kings and Queens. So many hopeless youths slipped through the cracks because no one was there to love them unconditionally.

The overwhelming poverty, illiteracy, and violence rates plagued a youth that had no hope for a future. Their role models were the American rappers that portrayed the glamourous lifestyle manifesting all pros and no cons to their gullible minds.

Noble looked at Ares and it was apparent what influence was most effective on him. His baggy jeans hung low, an over-sized New York Giants Jersey swallowed up his small frame, and a baseball cap turned backwards completed his wardrobe. A diamond **YGM** pendant hung from a white gold necklace around Ares' neck.

"You're smoking now?" Noble asked.

Ares took a pull off his joint before responding. "Yeah man. It's stressful times out here right now. I'm just trying to deal with the madness in the calmest way I can, ya know?"

"No, I don't know Ares. Look, I'm not going to lecture you about drugs, because now is not the time for that. We are all going through a tough time right now young man."

"Ya think?! Look around Noble. Haiti is messed up. Look at it man," Ares held his arms out and spun around. "Dead bodies piled up on every corner. People living in tents. There is barely any food and water, the governments been taken over −"

"Wait. What do you mean the governments been taken over?"

"Just like I said," Ares took more tokes off the joint. His eyes grew red and beady. Ares pulled some black sunglasses out of his pocket and sleekly put them on. He looked over at the over-crowded hospice and blew a gust of smoke in the air. "Slice is taking over. His Bête Noire is after carte-blanche. He's managed to turn the few officials who *had* backbones, against the people. Those that were already corrupt, willingly went along with his commands."

"Slice!" Noble said, scrunching up his face in disgust. The mere name left a bad taste in his mouth. Noble turned his head and spat on the ground.

"I've got my own thing now," Ares said, grabbing his pendant. "Young Goon Militia. Me and my boys are out here in our own lane. We aren't following Slice. If they wanna take over the government, us young goons are gonna take over the streets! They'll never see us coming."

Noble shook his head and put his hand on Ares' shoulder. "This is bigger than you and your little youth group."

"Youth group? You underestimate us and what we can do Noble."

"It's not that I underestimate you. You are a *very* smart young man. You should be focused on school and not some battle you can't win."

"School? Look around you man. Ain't no schools left! You must have forgotten what my name means. I was born to fight and go to battle for the people. You'll see," Ares declared.

Noble shook his head and patted Ares on top of his baseball cap. He knew the young man's parents well. They came from a long line of people named after Greek mythology figures. "I'll keep you in my prayers. Just be careful," Noble said and limped off.

The wheels in his head turned as he tried to think of what Slice was up to. Whatever it was, he knew it wasn't good. Slice was a plague. A virus. A pile of dog feces. Noble was so deep in thought that he didn't hear the soft voice behind him.

"Excuse me. Hi, sir. May I help you? Do you need anything?" Abby asked and tapped him on the shoulder. Noble jumped and almost fell off his crutches.

"Oh my, I'm so sorry," Abby said, wrapping her arms around his midsection while he caught his balance. "I didn't mean to startle you."

Noble looked at the woman he saw earlier. Her angelic smile was even more inviting up close. "It's alright. I'm fine," Noble said and steadied himself.

"You sure? I mean, I..." Abby trailed off.

"Something wrong?"

"You're the man Kiara told me about," Abby said.

"You know Kiara?" Noble asked with a piqued interest.

"Yes, I helped out at the General Hospital when I first got here. She showed me the ropes and we've become good friends. She told me about…" Abby looked at her feet.

"What? She told you about what?"

"Umm, never mind. It's a blessing to see you up and about." She stuck out her hand and introduced herself. "Hi, I'm Abby."

Her captivating smile froze Noble in his tracks. If it had been a commercial, there would have been a *ding* as the sun made her teeth gleam in the afternoon light. He took her hand in his and shook it.

"I'm Noblesse. But everyone calls me Noble."

"My, my, Noble. What a strong grip you have," Abby commented. Her southern drawl became more distinct and had a hint of flirtatiousness in it.

"Oh, I'm sorry about that, I didn't mean to —"

"Aww shucks, its ok Noblesse. Hmm, I like that name. Noblesse."

"Thank you. I like yours too."

"Well, actually its short for Abigail. Abigail Winters. But everyone calls me Happy Abby."

Noble took a step back and looked the friendly woman up and down. She stood about 5'6" in a body that was *all* woman. Tight blue jeans clung to her hips and thighs like a second skin. Her long brown hair was pulled into a ponytail. Abby's oval face suited her impeccably. Perfectly sculpted eyebrows framed hazel eyes that sparkled when she smiled. Shiny gloss coated her pink lips. She was a natural beauty that didn't need a drop of make-up to make a man's heart stop.

While Noble observed her, Abby canvassed the tall, hunk of man before her. At 6'3," Noble had lost a lot of weight in the hospital but was slowly gaining his muscle mass back. Abby looked at the bulging biceps that rippled from his chocolate-y skin as he tightly gripped his crutches. His broad chest extended from his body like a suit of armor. Gone was the cast on his leg and in its place was a walking boot that held his size 14 foot.

Abby looked at the high cheekbones that were so defined on his ebony face. She couldn't help but think he was the prototype for everything in the Couture world. His lips were full and soft looking. The last time she remembered them, they were dry. Now they were quite moist and very distracting.

When they locked eyes, Abby felt her cheeks fill with color as she blushed. He had the most gorgeous brown eyes she ever laid eyes on. Their whole exchange took three seconds, but it seemed like a lifetime. Especially since her embarrassment was clearly visible.

"Well, it's nice to meet you Happy Abby. I'll let you get back to your work."

"Ok. Well, I'll see you around I guess," Abby said, wondering if her blushing had scared him off. Noble saluted her and walked away.

A severely burned woman walked up to Noble as he hobbled along the street.

"Noble, we're so glad you're alive. Everyone heard about what happened to you. I was worried. I'm so sorry about Gen and the kids though."

"Thanks Dana. I'm trying to keep it together, but it's been hard. How are you doing?"

"Oh Noble, I'm in a lot of pain. I got burned all over my body. It's a miracle I survived!"

"What happened?"

"The house caught fire during the earthquake. I was cooking at the time and…"

"Oh Dana, that's terrible. I'm sorry," Noble said and hugged the woman. "My house burned down too. Telephone pole struck it and poof! My home is no more," he said.

"We've all suffered from this heartache. But we've got to hold on to our faith and pull together Noble. There's not much that *I* can do, but we need *you*."

"Me? What do you need me for?"

"Slice is taking over our country. He's even taken my husband into his stupid army."

"He's got Charles?" Noble asked in shock.

"Yes. He was so messed up over what happened to me that he believed all the garbage Slice put into his head. Now my husband is out somewhere rallying for an unjust cause with a machine gun in his hands and a bunch of hooligans."

"Wow, I'm sorry to hear that Dana. But what can I do? You know I'm not a fan of guns," Noble stated, looking distraught.

"Have you forgotten who you are? What you stand for? Noblesse oblige," Dana shouted, referring to the phrase that meant *the obligation of nobility to help those in dire need.*

Noble grimaced while she spoke to him.

"Why is everyone expecting *me* to save the world? I just lost my wife and kids! You are acting like I'm some super-human super-hero. I mean, look at me," Noble held his crutches out.

Dana put her small hand on his chest to calm him down. She lowered her voice to a more soothing tone. "Noble, you're right. I can only imagine the pain you're feeling in here right now," she patted his heart. "I don't mean to sound insensitive to your grief, but what's done is done. God called your family home. They're in a better place now." Dana bowed her head in a moment of silence before continuing.

"Think about how many lives will be destroyed if someone doesn't put an end to Slice. If you don't help, what is left of Haiti will be completely ruined. The entire island will erupt in chaos. The good are being corrupted as we speak. Even the sweet and innocent will turn bad. The youth will have an evil leader who will undoubtedly poison their gullible minds. I know how much you care for the youth Noble. Please, don't stand by and allow this country to go down in flames." Dana wiped a tear off her face and looked at him.

It was hard for Noble to look Dana in the eyes. Her entire body was covered in third-degree burns. The pink blistering of her skin looked like melted candle wax.

"Dana, when I get well, I'll do the best I can."

"That's all I ask for Noble. You may not think you're that great, but many of us consider you to be a super-hero."

"Aww, you're too kind," Noble smiled weakly.

Dana patted his chest again. "You have a genuine heart in here, so I know we will be alright."

Noble gave her a hug and watched Dana limp away. He stood there dumbfounded as he tried to process what she told him. He was torn. Feelings of pity, anguish, anger, and a great deal of empathy overwhelmed his soul as he looked around. *What am I gonna do? What in the world can I do?* he thought to himself.

Chapter 8

Rebuild or Rebel?

Noble was at a crossroads. As the days turned into nights, his once upbeat and positive demeanor turned distressingly sour. A black cloud hovered over his world. The hollowness in his soul was filled with pain, and it ate away at his sanity. He missed his children dearly. The sorrow and grief suffocated him. He had lost a few relatives over the years, including his parents, but no loss affected him so profoundly as this one.

The small tent he shared with the Lewis family didn't help matters much. The earthquake brought people from all walks of life closer together. It was inherent that an already close-knit family like the Lewis' would grow even closer because of the circumstances. Their nursing and bonding of one another was a constant reminder of what he no longer had; a *family*.

His *joie de vivre* (zest for life) was gone. He found himself grumpy and irritable. Noble began to snarl and bark at people like he was an alley mutt. So many people approached and badgered him about Haiti's current state, it took a toll on his attitude. He used that exasperation as fuel for his rehabilitation. He tripled his workout activities. He lifted cinder blocks and barrels of water to strengthen his limbs. This helped give his muscles more agility.

Everywhere he seemed to go, he saw Abby and her team dispensing food and supplies to displaced refugees. One day he went into town and observed her from afar. *Look at her. Do-gooder Americans come over here with their pity help and return to their rich American lives and families. What do they know about what we're going through?* Noble said to himself. The bitterness on his tongue was a harsh acerbity that was unbecoming of a man such as himself. He thought she could *feel* his thoughts, because she turned around and spotted him from 50 yards away. She smiled and waved. Her enthralling smile temporarily softened him. He acknowledged her with a quick head nod and turned his attention to a gimpy Labrador.

"Hey there boy," Noble said, patting the dog. "You ok buddy? I see you're limping. Did you mess your leg up in the earthquake boy?" The dog whimpered as Noble ruffled his fur. Noble bent down to examine the dogs wounded leg.

An hourglass shadow blocked his sunlight and he looked up.

"Aww, what do we have here?" Abby said and knelt beside him.

"Probably a fracture. He needs a splint."

"I can go get my medical kit −"

"No!" he cut Abby off. "I can take care of it. You go on about your business and continue your *charity* work."

Abby stood up and put a hand on her hip. "Excuse me?"

"That's what you're doing right, charity work?" Noble said, staring into her hazel eyes.

"This isn't 'charity' Noble. What is your problem? Did I upset you or something?"

"Look, I just want to be left alone ok? Now, if you want to continue your humanitarianism, I'll leave you to your benevolence."

"Benevolence?" Abby was puzzled. This was not the man she first met. The man who made her blush and gave her butterflies. He was distant, stand-offish, and cold-hearted towards her for some reason. Noble patted the dog, stood up and walked away without even telling Abby goodbye. She stood there appalled with her mouth open as he walked away.

A black SUV pulled in front of Noble. When the tinted back window rolled down, gusts of smoke wafted from inside the truck like a breathing dragon.

"You're a hard man to find Noblesse," a grim voice said.

"Slice. What can I do for you?"

"Get in. We need to talk."

"No thanks. Say what you have to say right here," Noble said defiantly.

"I don't speak my business in public like that Noblesse. That would be... Désagreablé." Laughter came from inside the vehicle.

"Slice, cut to it will you? I have important things to do."

"Ohhh, do you? Look who's more *edgy* now. You got a chip on your shoulder Nobe? Hmmm, I like that. Bête Noire is full of men with chips on their shoulders. That's a quality befitting of my organization. It makes us more ruthless."

"Impitoyable," someone from inside the SUV shouted.

Slice puffed on a blunt and continued. "Yeah, you know how I get down Noble. *Everybody* knows! I want you to join me Noble. With your skills, and my power, we can turn Haiti into a country to be reckoned with."

"Slice, I'm not into all that power and control stuff. I'm just an old construction worker."

"Old? Nah, not you Nobe. And you are more than a construction worker and you know it. Architect, engineer, the best in all of Haiti. You know you will be needed to rebuild this mess."

"I'm retired. I am physically unable to do what I used to Slice. I'm sorry, but I'm going into a new field."

"Ha!" Slice thought to himself, *you will be convinced when you find out what I have.*

"What are you going to do? Look around you. There are no jobs. Construction will be the number one demand," Slice said.

Just then, a reporter and her cameraman interrupted them.

"And how are you guys coping with this unimaginable tragedy?" the reporter said in her purple business skirt and blazer.

"Are you kidding me?" Noble said and pushed past her.

Slice blew smoke rings at the camera. "We'll talk another time Nobe," he yelled and rolled the window up. The SUV burned rubber, leaving the reporter to go annoy someone else.

Everywhere Noble went, he was reminded of what *was*. The many businesses and structures that he helped build were reduced to a heap of rubble.

His country was in shambles, and he was too emotionally paralyzed to care or do anything about it.

Bodies were still being discovered on a daily basis as special forces cleared the heavy ruins. They still had not removed all of the wreckage from Genevieve's school, so his wife and kids had yet to be found.

He constantly beat himself up as he recalled how the crazy Voodoo lady had warned him three years prior. She told him to take his family and go. To get out before the devastation occurred. Noble was a man of faith. He usually listened to the signs God sent him, but the one time he *should* have listened, he didn't; and it cost his family their lives.

"Why didn't I listen? Why the hell didn't I listen?!" he yelled to the sky.

"Listen to what?"

Noble spun around quickly with his fists raised. Abby took a couple of steps back and put her hands up in protest.

"Whoa, whoa, take it easy there, killer. I didn't mean to −"

"What are you doing here? Are you following me? Every time I turn around, I see *YOU*. What's with you?" Noble barked.

"Me? What's with *me?* I'm not the one with the problem," Abby said, getting into his face as her adrenaline pumped rampantly. "All I've done is be nice to you. But you treat me like crap every time I see you. I can understand that you're going through a difficult time, but that doesn't mean you have to take it out on the people trying to help you!"

"What do you know about a difficult time?" Noble scoffed. "What could you possibly know about what we're going through? You and your volunteers probably go back and eat steak every night after you do your charity work."

Abby turned beet red. "Listen, here, buster," she said, poking his chest with every word. "I'm not staying in some Hilton. I'm out here in the huts with the people. I'm eating beans out of the can, but I'm not complaining. I have not bathed in days! I probably smell like a barn," she said and smelled her armpit. "Whew!" Abby wrinkled her nose and continued. "Do I look like Sandra Bullock or Meryl Streep to you?"

"Who?" Noble asked puzzled.

"Never mind. The point I'm trying to make is, I am out here just like you. Just like *them*," Abby gestured to the many evacuees milling about. "I'm not some snobbish movie-star with her nose in the air. And I sure as heck ain't afraid to get my hands durrrty," her southern drawl came out. "I'm here because I care."

"Care? Yeah right. You don't care about us. You don't know the kind of pain we're going through. You don't know how we feel," Noble retorted.

"Why is that Noble because I'm a white woman? Do you think I'm some privileged chick that doesn't know about pain or loss? Well I've got news for you mister," Abby got in his face and poked his chest again. "You don't know me. You don't know squat! And to think, I actually prayed for you every day you were laid up in that hospital bed." Abby spun on her heels and stormed off fuming mad. Noble grabbed her arm before she got too far.

"Wait. What do you mean you prayed for me?" he asked incredulously. She looked down at his hand on her arm and he realized he was out of line. He quickly removed his hand. "I apologize."

"Wow, that's probably the nicest thing you've said to me thus far," Abby commented. Noble had to smile at that sly remark. That in turn made her smile.

"Why did you pray for me?"

Abby sighed loudly and folded her arms across her chest. "Because, when I saw you with all those tubes running out of your body, I felt a deep sense of grief."

"But why? It's not like I was the only injured Haitian there."

"I know that. My heart goes out to all of those who have been hurt. But it was something about you. Noble, you have this captivating aura that draws people in. I'm sure you know that, right?"

He did not answer her. He just stared at her and thought it was something about *her*, that made him forget about all his pain and troubles. He could sense her genuine care and concern.

"When Kiara told me about your family…" Abby trailed off as she choked up and began to cry. Noble didn't know whether to console her or leave her be. Instinctively he put an arm around her shoulder. Abby succumbed to his touch and rested her head on his chest.

"I know what it's like to lose the ones you love. I know what it's like to lose everything and have to rebuild your life from scratch. Trust me Noble, I *know*."

"Really?" he said, stroking her hair.

"Yes. Do you remember Hurricane Katrina in 2005?"

"Yes, isn't that the Hurricane that hit the southern parts of the U.S.?"

"Yes, it is. New Orleans felt it the most though. That's where I'm from Noble. New Orleans, Louisiana," Abby said. Her tears streamed more rapidly as she spoke. "I was three months pregnant with my first child. When the hurricane struck, it caused a massive pile-up on the interstate. I was able to get out of the car, but the city flooded so fast, I had nowhere to go. I used my car door that was knocked off as a raft. I received some serious injuries and lost my baby."

"Oh no Abby, I didn't know. I'm so sorry," Noble said, wrapping his arms around her. He gave her a big comforting bear hug.

"No need to apologize, it's not your fault," she sniffled. "Anyway, my fiancé, sister, brother, and many more family members perished in the hurricane. My house was completely destroyed. I lost everything I owned. I had to start over from scratch… literally."

Noble stroked her long silky hair. She looked up at him with pools of pain in her eyes. She *did* know. More than anyone else, Abby knew exactly what he was going through.

"That's why I volunteer my time whenever there's a natural disaster. No matter where it is; I'm there! I feel it is my obligation to give back to the people who experience these unspeakable acts. To have someone who has been through it is the relatable aspect that draws people like you and me together. We are the survivors who can offer hope while the depleted cope. *That's* why I do this Noble. For the people. I don't treat this as a charitable act. This is a serious cause that hits close to home for me."

It was in that moment, Noble knew he could love Abigail Winters. "Jeez Abby, I'm terribly sorry. I didn't know."

"How could you know? I mean, I don't blame you for being skeptical. All of these reporters roaming around, shoving microphones and cameras in people's faces and not lifting a finger to help. You probably saw me as some fat American woman looking to get her face on TV for doing an act of kindness."

"Fat? Umm…"

"Yes Noble, *fat*. You don't know what's under here," Abby pulled at her New Orleans Saint jersey. Noble could not see underneath her clothes, but he assumed whatever it was, it was probably a thing of beauty.

"Uh, yeah right. You my dear are far from fat. And if you *were,* you would still be an awesome person. I on the other hand, haven't been so awesome. I've been a jerk and I'm sorry. I just haven't been myself lately. To be honest with you, I hate what I've been turning into." Noble released Abby from his embrace and looked off into the distance. She whimpered softly, missing his comforting touch as soon as he pulled away. She was feeling something deeper than words could express for this man she barely knew.

"It has been extremely hard for me. My wife and kids were my world. And now they're gone. My house burned to the ground. Everything I ever had is in a pile of ashes." Noble began to tear up. Abby put a hand on his cheek and turned his face towards her.

"You poor thing. I am so very, very, sorry for your loss," she lightly stroked his cheeks.

"Bad things happen to good people all the time," Abby remarked. "It sucks, but it's reality. One thing I truly do believe, is that *everything* happens for a reason. Even when we don't understand why, there is a reason behind everything."

"Is it?" Noble asked uncertainly.

"Gosh yes. We may not know that reason right away, but in due time, God will reveal His purpose behind the things we cannot comprehend," Abby said as she looked into his eyes tenderly.

"I don't know Abby. I believe in God. I have tried my best to live a righteous and noble life. So why would He allow this to happen to me?"

"I can't answer that Noble. Only God can. Don't lose your faith over this. It's so easy to throw in the towel when you're down and out. But this is when you must be at your strongest. I almost gave up after Hurricane Katrina myself. If it weren't for my parents, who are deeply religious people, I don't know what I would've done. They helped me through it."

Noble tucked a strand of hair behind her ear. It was a slight gesture that came so natural to him. To her, it was an intimate pantomime that lit her insides on fire. She blushed a deep red.

"My parents were the same way," Noble said.

"Were? Did they —"

"Die in the earthquake? No. They passed years ago."

"Oh. I'm sorry," Abby said, and looked at her feet.

Noble placed his index finger under her chin and raised her head. "Don't be sorry. It's a part of life, right? They were good people. They lived a long, full life. Papa died of colon cancer, and mom passed two years later of natural causes. I think she died of a broken heart. After all, her partner of fifty-two years made her a widow. How could she go on without him?" They both stood in silence for a while. "The world is one big mystery."

"That it is. Life's a female dog; and then you die," Abby remarked.

Noble chuckled at her audaciousness. "You Americans have some peculiar sayings." Noble gazed into her hazel eyes and asked, "Is that one of your Sandra Pollock, Daryl Feet analogies?"

Abby burst out laughing. "No silly. It's Sandra *Bullock,* and Meryl Streep."

"Whatever! Who are they anyway?" Noble chuckled.

"Only two of Hollywood's finest actresses," she said demurely.

"Oh, no wonder I've never heard of them. I'm not really the celebrity following type."

"Understandable. Listen Noble, you have every right to mourn. I don't want that sorrow to destroy the good man that's inside of here," Abby said, tapping the left side of his chest. "No one or anything will *EVER* be able to replace your wife and children. But think about how they'd feel if they knew what you were becoming." Noble winced at that comment.

"Would they approve of you rebelling? I highly doubt that. I'm sure they would encourage you to do what you do best...build! And to rebuild with love, integrity, passion, honor, character and principle."

Noble couldn't deny it. Everything she said was true. "You're either a motivational speaker, or a teacher, which one are you?"

"Neither one," Abby laughed. "So, are you all for restoring Haiti back to its resilient self again with me?" Abby asked, extending her hand. He shook it and smiled.

"Yes, happy Abby, I'm with you!"

PART TWO

To Love Again

Chapter 9

Compassionate Companions

Only one word could describe their union: *fate*. Abby and Noble became inseparable. They spent their days side by side giving 110% into restoring Haiti. She was still part of her relief effort team, but most of her contributions were done with Noble.

He met her team and won them over with his genuine personality. They saw the connection between them and encouraged her to spend more time with him.

His health and agility recovered quickly. Those who knew how bad Noble was injured in the earthquake were amazed by his recuperation. He and Abby went to the hospital one morning where Kiara greeted them with a "kiss-kiss" (a Haitian reception where an air kiss is given to each cheek).

"How are you doing Noble? You're looking good. Bigger and stronger in fact," Kiara said, squeezing his bicep. Noble smiled and gave her a hug. "Oh Ki-Ki, I'm doing well. How about yourself?"

"Stressed as always, but maintaining," Kiara admitted. She turned to Abby and put her fists on her hips. "I'm mad at you miss thing. You haven't come to see me in forever." Kiara poked her lip out for effect, giving her best fake pout.

"I know, I know. I'm so sorry Kiara. Me and Noble have been so busy. There's not enough hours in the day to get the things done that need to be done."

"Don't I know it honey!" Kiara exclaimed as she looked from Abby to Noble and back again. *Hmpf, they **DO** look good together*, she thought to herself.

"What's with the big goofy smile Ki-Ki?" Noble asked.

"Ohhhh, nothing," Kiara sang playfully. Abby squinted her eyes at Kiara. Call it a woman's intuition, but she knew what Kiara was thinking. Noble and her were just friends, and she didn't want Kiara or anyone else to get the impression that they were more than that.

Abby and Noble had been standing shoulder to shoulder, but Abby took a few steps to her right to distance herself socially.

"I heard you two were going around the city helping out. I knew you'd eventually find time to visit little ol' us over here," Kiara said with a smile.

"Oh puh-lease," Abby responded. "You know it's not even like that Kiara."

"Yeah Ki-Ki, don't be saying that. We brought gifts for little ol' you over here," Noble remarked with a grin.

"Gifts? What cha bring?" Kiara perked up excitedly.

"Come find out," Abby said and grabbed Kiara's hand. They walked to the entrance where dozens of boxes of medicine filled the doorway.

"Thank the Lord!" Kiara praised, throwing her hands in the air. She read the labels on the boxes. Morphine, Ketamine, and various anesthetics filled the boxes Kiara inspected. Her hospital was in desperate need of those supplies. "You guys are saviors."

"Don't thank us. We're just the delivery men," Noble said. Abby cleared her throat loudly and gave Noble a look. "Oh, my bad. Delivery man and *woman*," he corrected himself.

Kiara smiled and picked up a box. "Come on you two, help me bring this stuff inside."

They put the medical supplies up and assisted Kiara with several patients. The conversation flowed organically as they caught each other up to speed on their current lives. The mood turned dark when Kiara brought up Slice.

"He's been terrorizing the streets Noble. His regime is growing rapidly. The people are afraid. Everyone is on edge, and when it erupts…" Kiara shivered and got lost in her own thoughts.

"I know Ki-Ki," Noble sighed loudly and shook his head. "That…that bastard is ruthless."

Abby heard much talk about the notorious Slice. She had yet to see him though. Not only had Noble warned her about him, many of the Haitians she encountered murmured not so pleasant things about him. Nicole and Hailey told her just the sight of Slice had scared the crap out of them. Abby had no room for negative or nefarious people in her life. If it wasn't positive and uplifting, she wanted nothing to do with it.

"Hey, you guys, how about a break? Let's grab a bite to eat," Abby said. Kiara and Noble suddenly became hungry at the mention of food and agreed to some lunch.

✻✻✻✻

Later that evening after a long day's work, Noble took Abby to a secluded Bay area overlooking the ocean. It was one of his favorite spots on the island. A place of peace and solitude. It was the first time since the earthquake that he had returned there. They were the only two people there. It was a very dark night, but the moon shone down on the water, illuminating the bay with vibrant light. Noble and Abby sat against a tree and took their shoes off.

"Ahh, this is leisurely," Abby gasped. It felt good to sit still for a minute. They had been going non-stopped and often neglected breaks. She was short of breath and sore but didn't want to complain.

"Indeed, it is," Noble responded. They sat in silence and enjoyed the view. They listened to the waves and surrendered to the state of relaxation that enveloped them.

"I know this may sound cliché, but do you come here often?"

Noble looked at her. The moon cascaded over her pretty face. He smiled and she smiled back. He returned his attention back to the water. Clear and blue as far as the eyes could see. Other islands like Cuba and Jamaica were not far from their vantage point.

"Yes Abby. I used to come here often. This is probably the most historical piece of land in all of Haiti. This is where former slave Toussaint L' Ouverture led a successful revolt on slavery, helping Haiti become the first Latin American state to achieve its independence in 1804. It started in 1791, so it was a long-fought battle that caused hundreds of thousands of deaths, including Toussaint's who died in prison in 1803. It was the first revolution of its kind. It established an independent nation built on resilience, courage, and bravery."

"Wow, I didn't know that."

"Not many people outside of us Haitians do. We were the first black republic that gave hope to the oppressed Africans everywhere. That freedom and sovereignty was not only a dream to them, it was a goal that was very much accomplishable. Several wars started and ended on this very Bay. This is where Christopher Columbus visited in 1492, and according to my great-great grandmother, this quiet piece of land is where the earliest settlers first came up with the Creole language."

"Dang, really?" Abby asked incredulously. She was enjoying the history lesson he gave her.

"Yes. Many people consider Creole to be the language for the poor and uneducated, while French is seen as the 'rich man's tongue.' But when Haiti was first established, Creole was *thee* vernacular. It got overshadowed by something more current and popular, like most things in history."

"What do you mean?" Abby asked confused.

"Well, take the earthquake for example. It received much national coverage right after it struck, but the donations and prayers will decrease each week that passes, while current news takes over the headlines and this devastation becomes just another memory and statistic for the record books."

Noble sounded like a History teacher giving a lesson to his students. Abby remembered that his wife was a teacher and that he came from a very educated background, so his knowledge wasn't too surprising to her. Abby nodded in agreement. As sad as it was, Noble was speaking the truth. It was the way of the world. A world where everything is so fast-paced and ADD, not much can hold one's attention long enough to keep them from moving on to the "next thing" or fixation.

Noble heard a sniffle and looked over at Abby. There was a dam pooling in her pretty eyes that threatened to burst. He put a comforting arm around her shoulder, that is when she melted like warm butter. All the pain and emotions she'd bottled up came pouring out. Abby sobbed deeply and Noble scooped her up in his big, strong arms and hugged her tenderly. She balled her eyes out, soaking his shirt with tears that went on forever.

Abby allowed her vulnerability to flow freely, no longer caring about portraying the strong independent woman with a guard up. Noble was right there for her when she truly needed someone to open up to, and she was grateful for his presence.

She didn't know why she was fighting her true feelings for this man. She knew how she felt, and it was more than just a friendship interest.

"Let it all out Abby, don't hold back," Noble said and kissed the top of her head. He felt her body convulse in his arms. Her cries and sobs were muffled in his chest as he lovingly stroked her back. His feelings for her were a constant reminder of the family he just lost. Falling in love so quickly and under such circumstances made him feel incredibly guilty.

Holding her in his arms and absorbing her pain made him feel needed. Not wanted but **needed**. That was an incredible feeling for someone who'd just lost everything. He doubted

Abby knew how deeply he cared for her, and he didn't want to play his cards just yet. He intended on keeping things platonic and not stepping out of the "friend zone." When those quiet moments lingered a bit too long and began to border on the lines of intimacy and passion, he'd check himself and pull back.

After encouraging Abby to let it all out, Noble released her from his grasp and held her at arms-length. She swiped at her tears and smiled.

"You must think I'm the biggest cry baby in the world," Abby sniffled and wiped her nose.

"Huh? No, not at all. Emotions are meant to be expressed. When you're happy, you smile. When you're sad, you cry. That's how it's supposed to be."

"What does one do when they feel…guilty?" Abby asked.

"Guilty? What would you have to feel guilty about?"

"Oh, I don't know. Lots of things. Stuff that is out of my control makes me feel sheepish inside."

"Hmpf," Noble grunted and stroked his chin. He couldn't tell her he had feelings of guilt himself. *Heed my advice and re-write history.* He'd been warned but didn't take the lady in red seriously.

"So?"

"So, what?" Noble replied.

"What does one do when we're guilty?" Abby asked. "If we cry when we're sad, and smile when we're happy, what do we do when we're guilty?"

Noble studied her for a moment. His deep brown eyes penetrated her soul. He cocked his head to the side and looked at her round face. It was so cute and inquisitive. Unable to resist any longer, he cupped her face in the palms of his hands.

"You have the softest, roundest −"

"Hey, you haven't even touched them yet, how would you know?" Abby said teasingly. For a moment Noble was confused until he saw her look down at her bosom and smile sheepishly. He laughed lightly at her candid humor and got back on track.

"Face! The softest, roundest *face*. It's almost like…like a pie," Noble commented.

"Great, now I'm fat with a pie face. Gee, thanks a lot *Noble*."

"Huh? For one thing, you are far from fat. You are thick and sensationally curvaceous to say the least. And pie face? Well, that's kind of a nice nickname for you. Everyone calls you Happy Abby, I want something only *I* call you. Yes, I think I like that. Pie face," he said, stroking her cheek with the back of his hand. Abby melted inside. The term of endearment nickname he gave her, and his touch, made her feel soft and gooey inside. Her eyelashes fluttered like butterfly wings.

"Well, I guess so. But that doesn't mean you get to eat my face though mister," she joked. "So, don't be getting any ideas."

Noble raised his hand. "Cross my heart and hope to *pie*." They both burst out laughing.

Chapter 10

It's So Hard To Say Goodbye

Abby felt light-headed and dizzy. She'd been short of breath and sore more frequently. She chalked her fatigue and swollen limbs up to the hard labor she had put in.

"You alright girl? You look a little pale," Hailey asked.

"Yeah, I'm fine. Just a little parched is all," Abby responded as she fanned herself.

"Well, you don't look alright. Maybe you should sit down and take a load off for a bit, you have been going non-stopped," BJ said when he walked up to her.

"You guys are over-reacting. Just get me a bottle of water and I'll… I'll —" before she could finish her sentence, Abby fainted.

When she came to, the whole gang was around her. Hailey, Eric, BJ, Nicole, Tim, and Noble were all smiling down warmly at her. She was brought to Kiara's hospital where they attended to her medical needs.

"You should go back home for a couple of weeks and rest Abby. Eat some decent food, fill up on fluids, and relax. I'll send your lab work in and let you know the results as soon as I get them. Your field team said this is your third time fainting in a matter of days."

"Yeah, I've been feeling icky. I don't know why," Abby responded somberly. She hoped she wasn't coming down with anything serious. She knew Kiara was right though, she was putting a serious strain on her health. The lack of proper nutrition and rest was clearly taking its toll on her well-being.

"You've been a big help to us all, but you're no good to us if you're sick Abby. Take my advice and just go home for a few weeks," Kiara said.

"Yeah, I know. You're right. It's just —"

"You don't want to leave Noble," Kiara interrupted her with a true statement.

Abby looked at Kiara and nodded. "He's lost so much already. I just feel like I'm all he's got right now."

Kiara nodded in agreement. "In some ways, you're right. Having you by his side keeps the pain of losing his family at bay. I mean, he'll never be the same again. None of us will. But you're helping him deal with his loss significantly just by being you Ms. Happy Abby."

That made Abby smile a sincere heartfelt beam. As much as being a missionary and helping people meant to her, she knew she'd be no good to no one in her current condition. Especially Noble. "How will I tell him?"

"Just be honest with him. He's a reasonable man, I'm sure he'll understand. And hey, it's not like you're leaving *forever*. You will come back, won't you?"

"You better believe it! My work is far from done here," Abby said and they both hugged.

****

It was a silent ride to the airport. They were both lost in their own thoughts. What transpired the night before was still fresh.

Noble carried her luggage to the terminal where he finally cleared the air. "I'm deeply sorry for blowing up like that last night."

"Oh Noble, it's ok."

"No, it is *not* ok. Abby, I'm an honorable man. A respectful man who treats women with the highest regards. I was completely out of line, and I apologize. I... I'm under so much pressure, and I'm still trying to cope with all of this," he made a sweeping motion with his arms. The over-populated airport was full of displaced families and relief effort teams. He didn't want to admit the feelings that were growing stronger and stronger for her by the hour.

"It was selfish of me to not consider your health and the fact that you did have a life before little old Haiti crumbled." He mustered a slight smile, but his eyes were sad.

She took his hands in hers before she spoke. "Noblesse, you are the kindest, bravest, strongest, sweetest, sincerest man that I have **EVER** met. We are more than just passing friends. Our bond—whatever that may entail—will last a lifetime. As soon as

I get myself back to 100% I will be back as soon as I can to help you rebuild your country. Okey dokey smokey?"

Noble had to smile at her little dorky sayings. It wasn't long until her flight announced it was boarding. They embraced in a warm hug that seemed to last forever. Abby stood on her tip toes and rested her face on his shoulders. Her tears silently dampened his shirt as Nobles hands palmed the small of her back. He hugged her tightly like he was never going to see her again. In some strange way, in the back of his mind, he thought he never would, and he didn't want to let her go. He hoped through some magical force, that their souls would intertwine during their hug. That way, they could carry around a piece of each other forever and always.

Abby kissed his cheek softly as they finally let go of each other. As strong as Noble was, it was a losing battle trying to fight the lone tear that spilled from his right eye. Abby swiped it up with her thumb before it could get far. She promised to keep in touch and be back as soon as possible. They said their final goodbyes and Abby vanished into the terminal.

Noble walked to the window and pressed his face against the glass as he watched her plane gear up for take-off. His tears rolled down the windowpanes like silent raindrops.

He saw Abby press her face in the small airplane windows. When she put her palm to the glass, he followed suit. When his full lips pursed against the glass, sending her a long distant kiss, she did the same from her tiny square window.

Abby's plane took off down the runway. When it was no longer visible, Noble felt those familiar pangs of emptiness that he felt weeks ago. He felt like he lost all he had left… again.

Chapter 11

When It Rains It Pours

Abby arrived at the Louis Armstrong International Airport extremely jet lagged. With her recent bouts of fainting and not eating much, her sluggish feeling after flying high was zombie-like. She walked through the airport like an extra in the Thriller video. Her chest was sweaty and sticky, she desperately craved a bubble bath.

When Abby got to baggage claim, she sighed in irritation because of the long line. "Is that the room where the players dwell?" a big man with coke bottle glasses walked up and asked her.

"Excuse me?" Abby replied confused.

"Your shirt." he pointed to the Haiti T-shirt she wore. 1-12 was written on it. "The singing group, 112. You remember them? Is that the roo —"

"Prince, are you bothering this young lady?" a woman with gray hair walked up and asked. "I'm terribly sorry about my son miss."

"Oh, it's ok. He was asking something about my shirt."

"Yeah ma, her shirt…don't you remember 112?"

"Boy, I have no clue what you're talking about. But you can't be bothering folks like that."

"No, it's fine," Abby said, realizing that the man was challenged in some way. "I got this from Haiti. It means January 12th. The day the earthquake happened."

"Ohhhh, my bad," the guy said shaking his head.

"Ma'am you have to excuse my son. He has brain cancer, so he has outbursts at times and doesn't always make sense."

"Oh God, I'm so sorry," Abby said in shock, throwing her hands to her mouth.

"Oh, don't be honey, it's not your fault. Just another curve ball life throws our way," the old woman said. "This is my son Prince, and I'm Darla."

Abby shook their hands. "Nice to meet you both, I'm Abby."

"I have tubes in my head Abby. See?" Prince lowered his head and rubbed on his wrinkly scalp.

"Prince, don't nobody want to keep looking at your head boy. You're supposed to be looking for our bags. I'm sorry about that Abby, he just... " Darla trailed off as she looked at her son and shook her head sadly.

"Hey, it's ok, really. So, is he alright? Or... "

"Well this is his second battle with brain cancer. They got most of it. They put shunts in so parts of his brain that *can* get oxygen, will receive it through special tubes."

Abby gasped in horror.

"Child, it's ok. We have today right? That's why we're here in New Orleans. Prince always had Mardi Gras on his Bucket list, so I got us a whole week stay. We're gonna see the town and take pictures of all the places he wants to go," Darla shrugged and looked at her son. The look in her eyes was a mixture of intense sadness and sparkling hope.

"Well that's awesome. I hope you enjoy your time in the big easy," Abby told them.

"Ha haaa, that's what they used to call me back in my player days," Prince commented and rubbed his palms together.

"Is that so?" Abby said with a big smile. "Umm, Bourbon street can get kind of intense for tourists, so just be careful when you're down there," Abby informed them and patted Prince's shoulder. He smiled and drool ran from his mouth.

"Thank you. I will keep that in mind. Come on Prince, there goes our bag," Darla pointed to a ragged shiny blue vinyl suitcase. Small pieces of clothing sprouted from the bag as Prince lifted it from the baggage carousel. He walked to his mother and sat the suitcase down.

He looked at Abby and said, "Never give up. No matter what you go through in life, as long as there is still breath in your lungs, never give up hope, and chase your dreams." He gave her a curtsy bow and scurried off.

"Thank you. God bless!" Abby yelled after them as she waved goodbye.

✷✷✷✷

Being in Haiti gave Abby a better perspective of real-life rural areas that were neglected. People were acting out because they were wounded − physically, emotionally, financially, and spiritually. The taxi rode through the inner-city and Abby looked at the constant barrage of boarded up houses covered in Graffiti. She shook her head in disgust and sadness. Hurricane Katrina hit years ago, and her city still hadn't picked up the pieces to rebuild certain areas. They needed their own Noble in New Orleans.

Noble. She smiled when she thought of him. So strong. So smart. So handsome. A *REAL* man. A unique specimen like non-other. She could feel her neck and face flushing. She quickly looked to see if the cab driver was watching her through the rearview mirror. He wasn't.

The closer she got to her place, the more she felt like something wasn't quite right. The hairs on the back of her arms and neck stood up. The eerie feeling in the air usually came to her when danger was present. It was the same feeling she had the day Katrina hit, and the night she got mugged in college.

After tipping the taxi driver, Abby exhaled and looked at her building. *Home sweet home.* She entered her humble abode and dropped her luggage in the foyer. She curled up on the sofa and sorted through her pile of mail. While separating the junk mail from the important stuff, Abby picked up the phone to check her voicemail messages.

"Abby, please call me right away, Renee is in the hospital," her friend Kim screamed. Abby dialed her immediately.

"Abby? Oh, Thank God. I didn't know when you'd be back."

"Yeah Kim, I just got home not too long ago. What's wrong with Renee? What happened?"

"Abbs, I don't know how to tell you this… but Renee has stage 4 cancer. The tumor has spread to her bones and brain. She's deteriorating fast," Kim sobbed.

"Oh my God!" Abby gasped in shock and dropped the phone in her lap. She shakily picked it back up. "Where is she?"

"University. She wants to see you. Want me to come get you? That way we can go together."

"Yes please. Give me a half hour to shower and get myself together."

"It's gonna be at least that. I have to drop Steve off at his Dad's. I'll be there in like an hour ok?"

"Sure, sounds good," Abby said and disconnected. *Dear God, please have mercy on Renee*, she silently prayed.

The car ride to the hospital was a quiet one while Abby tried to digest the information about her good friend's condition. It's as if everyone close to her suffered some sort of fatality in one way or another. Cancer was a major disease taking out those she loved dearly. She thought back to the man at the airport whose last wish was to visit the Big easy. *Prince*. She smiled sadly and shook her head. There was a four-letter expletive for how she felt about the big C.

Abby and Kim walked three flights of stairs to get to Renee's room. When they entered, she was resting. The machine she was hooked up to beeped steadily. Abby had been in so many hospitals she was accustomed to the eeriness that came when one entered a patients' room. But to see her good friend in such a broken and fragile shell brought her to tears.

"Oh Renee," Abby sobbed and threw herself across her dying friends' torso. Her tsunami's worth of tears was a contagious drift. Kim erupted in a flood of grief too as she grudgingly strode to the bed.

"Come on Abby, you can't be throwing yourself…" Kim grabbed Abby by the shoulders, trying to pull her off Renee's tiny frame. "Gosh, how much weight have you lost? You're a bag of bones," Kim exclaimed.

"Huh? Oh, Kim, stop it. I haven't lost any weight," Abby sniffed and wiped her nose with the back of her hand.

"Um, unless they have Thrive in Haiti, I don't know how you can't see the significant difference. I mean, look at what you're wearing. Everything looks so… *baggy* on you. I'm used to your attire *painting* your curves."

Abby looked down at her outfit. Her once tight blue jeans were loose on her, and her blouse was unusually big. *Hmm, maybe she's right.* Abby paced the foot of her friend's hospital bed and massaged her temples. She thought she was dizzy from the stress and lack of rest.

"Abbs, maybe you should sit down, you look pale honey," Kim commented.

"Pale? Pale? Oh, come on, I've been in Haiti smoldering in the sun. I'm as tan as your famous dinner rolls," she joked light-heartedly. Abby didn't make it to the chair before she collapsed on the floor.

When she came to, she was in a hospital bed next to her friend who was now awake. Kim was standing over Abby holding a cold washcloth against her forehead. A nurse and doctor were also at her bedside.

"Hello Ms. Winters, I'm Dr. Grolling," the tall George Clooney-ish looking man said as he extended his hand. Abby shook it weakly and smiled.

"Seems as if you fainted and took a pretty nasty spill to the noggin. I'm afraid you might have a concussion. We're going to run some tests on you if that's ok?"

Abby had a splitting headache that throbbed harder and harder with each syllable the man spoke. The doctor ran through a list of questions, from her appetite, to how much sleep she'd been getting. Kim interjected about Abby having lost at least 20 pounds since the last time she saw her. The nurse nodded and made some notes on her clipboard.

After the questions were answered, she informed them of her recent stint in Haiti, where the dizzy spells and fainting began.

"It could just be fatigue, but we'll do some tests anyway," Dr. Grolling stated.

"I was going to see my doctor in a few days anyway, could it wait until then?" Abby asked.

"Who's your doctor?"

"Dr. Bearer."

"Big Bear?" Dr. Grolling smiled.

"You know him?"

"I do. We went to school together. He graduated a year before me. He's a good guy."

"Yeah…"

"Well, if you feel like it can wait —"

"Abby, you don't look so good. For Pete's sake, you're already *here*. What if it's something serious?" Kim said.

"Yeah Abbs, look at me," Renee spoke for the first time and coughed rapidly. "If I would have come earlier..." she coughed so hard the nurses rushed to her aid.

"Take it easy Renee," Kim urged. "Abbs, she has a point. Let them run some tests on you please."

"Ok, ok. Since I'm here already, why not? Alright doc, do what you've gotta do."

After they drew blood, they told her they'd call her with the results within a week. That dreaded phone call revealed she had Non-Hodgkin's Lymphoma. Her heart dropped to the pit of her stomach listening to the doctor describe her disease.

"Your white blood cells have been compromised, forming abnormal lymphocytes. The good news is, we caught it early and can treat it in various ways. We will start you on a medication that will kill the pre-cancerous cells that have been detected. Once you complete the three-week cycle, you'll go on two more medications. Those will help your body make new white blood cells."

"Will I be Ok? I'm not gonna die, am I?" Abby asked sadly.

"No. no, Ms. Winters. I can assure you that you will be fine. Your condition isn't as serious as say, your friend Renee," he admitted truthfully. "There are always complications and risks involved when treating any disease, but the odds are definitely in your favor," he said soothingly.

"Don't worry Abbs, we'll get through this," Kim grabbed her hand and squeezed it.

Abby smiled and bowed her head. *Why me? Will my misfortune ever end?* When she looked up, she saw people who wanted healing and love. She wasn't alone. She was thankful for the friends and loved ones she could depend on. A lot of people weren't as lucky as she was.

"You're right. As long as there is breath in my lungs, I'll never give up hope!"

Chapter 12

The Return

As the weeks went by, she grew incredibly frustrated that she had not heard from Noble. With the telephone lines in disarray, she had to resort to snail mail. She'd written Noble several letters and mailed them to Kiara's clinic. They were never returned to her, so she assumed that he got them. *Why hadn't he responded?*

"Another letter from the white woman came for Noble," one of Slice's goons said. He handed his boss the envelope.

Slice reclined in his chair and puffed a cigar. He looked at the envelope addressed to *Noblesse L' Ouverture* in his hands. He thought of how close Noble and Abby had become while she was in Haiti. He shook his head and set the letter on fire. He and his degenerates laughed at his fire show display. He tossed the flaming ball of feelings into the wastebasket.

The Regime had taken over several governmental compounds, including the Post office. They were intercepting and destroying mail by the bin load. They were heartlessly stealing the checks from sympathetic souls from around the world.

"That woman is gonna cause us some problems," Slice said as he peeled a papaya with a curvy-bladed hunting knife.

"You really think so boss?" one of his flunkies asked and scratched his head.

"Yeah, they got really close while she was here. She wormed her way into his heart while he was vulnerable." Slice hissed.

"What's Vernon blow?" the dumb boy said. Slice threw half of his papaya at the kid and it hit him in the eye.

"Vulnerable, ya dummy! It means at your lowest. He was messed up in the head behind losing his family. The man wasn't in his right mind."

"Ohhh, he was coo-coo," the clueless boy replied.

Good help is hard to find Slice thought to himself and shook his head. "You guys are dumber than the dumbest of dumbery!

Jeez, look. If he does what he's told, and oversees my project, I might let him be with the American woman. Either way, he'll do what I tell him to do for the Queen of hearts." Slice laughed sadistically and his followers mimicked him with their own cackles and grunts. "Somebody get me another papaya!" he ordered and kicked his feet up.

✻✻✻✻

"I knew you'd be here," her voice sing-songed in the air. It was late, so the city was silent. Every word made his heart skip beats while the butterflies in his stomach twerked in the pit of his belly. He didn't want to turn around for fear there'd be nothing there but the wind. He had been dreaming of her a lot lately, maybe he was hearing voices now.

The crunch of misty grass being stepped on erased his hearing voices theory. This was no figment of his imagination. "Mmmmm, I've missed you," Abby moaned into his back. She came from behind and slid her arms between his, placing her hands on his chest. Every beat of his heart pulsated from her palms to other parts of her body.

Noble closed his eyes and allowed the sweet smell of her Daisy Love Perfume to intoxicate his nostrils. He put his hands over hers and could feel the heat beneath her skin radiating through his own palms. They both moaned simultaneously. Noble turned and faced her.

"You didn't answer any of my letters. I thought...I don't know, I thought maybe you had forgotten about me," Abby shrugged and looked at her feet.

"Letters? I never got any letters. What are you talking about?"

"The ones I sent to the clinic. I even sent some in Kiara's name. Gosh, I musta sent about a dozen of 'em! You mean to tell me you didn't get one single letter from me?" Abby asked with a raised eyebrow.

"No, I didn't. And I see Kiara every day. We talk about you often, wondering if we'd ever hear from you again," Noble admitted.

"Wow, really? Noble you and Kiara have got to know I'm not just a love 'em and leave 'em type of gal. I meant it when I said I was going to come back. Even against doctor's orders, I wasn't gonna —"

"Wait, what Doctor's orders?"

"Oh, it's nothing really Noble. We'll talk about it later. I want to know what's going on with you. I see you're getting your muscles back," she said and squeezed his biceps. They jumped like anacondas in her warm palms and she blushed.

Noble sighed wearily. "Everything is in such disarray here. There is no order. There is no structure. The government has been compromised, and there is *still* no peace. I'm doing everything I can, but I'm only one man." Noble walked toward the tallest pile of bricks and stood on them.

"Slice has seemed to weasel himself into a high position of power."

"Ugh!" Abby's body shivered at the thought of that monstrous reptile that she despised. "So, besides scumbag, how is everything? Is Kiara ok?"

"Yes, she's fine. Overworked as always, but as you know, she won't have it any other way. Wow, I still can't believe you're here Pie face," Noble said smiling big.

There he goes again, turning me into mush, Abby thought to herself. Noble rested his forearms on top of Abby's shoulders and stared into her hypnotic hazel eyes. She could feel the heat rush to her face and ears when he looked at her the way he did. "Well, believe it mister. I'm here, in the flesh! Did ja miss me?"

"I sure did," Noble exclaimed and hooked the small of her back. He drew her to him closely. When Noble leaned down, she closed her eyes and tilted her head back in eager anticipation. A soft moan, barely above a whisper, escaped her lips. Abby's arms went around his waist like a belt, and he welcomed the squeeze.

With his free hand, Noble stroked her temples with his fingertips before they combed through her hair tenderly. He cupped the nape of her neck and pulled her close.

His warm breath teased her lips with gusts of promise. Her body begged, pleaded and practically *screamed,* for him to claim her as his, but his approach was a gentle courting that made her yearn for him even more.

Noble brushed the tip of his round nose back and forth across hers and breathed ever so lightly across her lips. Abby swore he could hear her swallow the lump in her throat because of how quiet it was outside. A light breeze blew her hair into the wind and Noble parted his lips. Abby whimpered the closer he got to her. When their lips finally connected, it was like the 4th of July! Fireworks ignited within their souls and made for a fiery explosion of love, lust, and longing.

The kiss was slow and passionate. It was equal parts give, and equal parts take. Abby feasted on his full lips that looked and tasted like sweet plums. Noble sucked on her lips in between passionate pecks and savored them as if they were appetizers.

Being the self-less givers that they were, they both wanted to make the intimate exchange more pleasurable for the other.

This resulted in a dynamic dance of calculated lips that smacked while their tongues explored hungrily. Their noses brushed back and forth like windshield wipers, as their heads alternated from side to side in a rhythmic fashion.

A deep, guttural moan came from the back of Abby's throat. Noble took that as a good sign and pulled her closer. She was floating in bliss, her enthusiastic moans solidified this while her hands caressed his body. Just when Abby thought she would melt into a puddle of goo, Noble gently pulled back, sucking on her bottom lip until it escaped his grasp. Abby slowly opened her eyes and the smile on her face was like none he'd ever seen.

"Wow!" they said at the same time and laughed.

"That was the best kiss of the century!" Abby exclaimed.

"Of the century? I'd say of all time!"

"Yeah, you're probably right. My bad," Abby said with a laugh. She fanned herself. "Woo!"

Noble scooped her into his arms and hugged her tightly. "How did you know where to find me?" he asked and kissed the top of her head.

"Well, I know this bay area is one of your favorite places to go, especially at night. So, I came here first, and got lucky... in more ways than one," Abby said with a seductive wink.

"Oh woman, you are something else!"

****

Ares leaned against a three-story brick building. His Young Goon Militia (YGM) crew huddled around a portable boombox that sat on a milk crate.

"It's about to get ugly y'all. They've taken over every arm of government. Everyone is too afraid to go against Slice and his regime, they are joining the Bêta Noire in droves," Ares said.

"We're the opposition now. And because we're young, they sleep on us. They underestimate us because they think we're young and dumb. Ha! We'll see about that. No matter the devastation we suffered because of the earthquake, we *cannot* let Slice destroy what our ancestors built. We are a country of strength and pride, most importantly, we are a country of survivors!" The young men cheered and high-fived each other in agreement.

"I'm not gonna stand by and watch that turd set us back 100 years. We're nobody's slaves! We're not his puppets! No, we will fight to the death if need be. All in the name of Haiti!"

"Haiti!" YGM shouted proudly.

"*We* are the future. Not *them*. It's up to us to do whatever we have to do to protect Haiti."

"Protect Haiti!" the eager young men shouted. Ares wrapped up his motivational pep talk. He informed them that they must act in silence and remain under the radar while they recruited more young people for their movement.

"There is strength in numbers. So, while we gain more goons secretly, we will play like we are following Slice's Regime. Truth be told, by the time Bête Noire finds out about our plan of action, it will be too late for them," Ares said and laughed loudly.

"All of you are expected at target practice for two hours a day. When it's time to pick them off one by one, I don't want *any* mishaps. Stay sharp, and always be alert."

YGM nodded as they soaked up the knowledge from their fearless leader. They were young wolves in sheep's clothing. Determined to not let their country get overtaken by the corrupt and evil ones.

Chapter 13

Shock & Awe

Noble took a step back and admired the work they put into the new Church. "Things are coming along nicely, don't you think?" he said to Abby.

"Oh my God, are you kidding me? This is beyond awesome!" she gushed. "And thanks for including me in the garden project," she pointed to the beautiful array of flowers that canvassed the front of the building.

"Pssh, it was your idea to have something nice for people to look at that wouldn't remind them of the pain and destruction. I would much have rather put a statue of *you* out front, but I think some people might have questioned that," Noble joked.

Abby playfully hit him in the arm. "Aww shucks, you're making me blush."

Noble tucked a loose strand of hair behind her ear and smiled. "Good, I'm doing my job then."

She bit her lip and looked at her feet. *It's time.* "Noble... I, I'm leaving."

He looked at his watch. "Oh, I guess it is about lunchtime eh? What cha having? Want some company?"

"No, Noble. I mean, I'm *leaving* leaving. As in, leaving Haiti and going back home."

Noble felt like a horse kicked him in the chest. He looked at her in disbelief. Abby stared at her shoes and wrung her hands to avoid seeing the pain in his eyes. He placed a finger beneath her chin and raised her head slowly. Abby held her eyes tightly shut to prevent the obvious. Noble saw the tears she tried so desperately to prevent from surfacing.

"When?"

Abby hesitated while she swallowed her sobs. "Day after tomorrow."

Noble spun around and put his hands in his pockets. He looked at the structure he built from the ground up and tried to smile. Inside he was seething, and his heart was broken like shattered glass. Even though there were sounds of heavy machinery operating, jackhammers drilling, mopeds zooming to and fro, the silence between the two of them was deafening. Abby chewed on her lip until she tasted blood. She stepped forward and put a hand on his shoulder. He coldly shrugged it off and stepped away from her.

"When were you going to tell me?"

Abby shrugged to herself, looking at the back of his head. "Noble, I'm not well. You know this. I have to go home and see my doctor. I've gotta get some rest. I —"

"When… were… you… going… to… tell me?!"

"I don't know. It never seemed like the right time. I wanted to finish a few more projects like we discussed, but I haven't been feeling the greatest, so I arranged a flight a few days ago."

Noble turned around and faced her. "So, you knew you were leaving for a while and didn't tell me?"

Abby wanted to return her guilty eyes back to the ground but the look on his face held her in a shameful trance. "Sort of. I've been kind of undecided, but some of the team has been suggesting I go home."

"Yeah right!" Noble snorted. "You're just like everyone else. Come do your little charity work and leave before it's completed because you can't handle the conditions!"

"Noble, that's not true!"

"Get the hell away from me!" he yelled, surprising them both. He stepped back and took some deep breaths.

"Noble, what good am I if I keep passing out every hour?"

"You're a faker! You're just trying to get out of here, so you fake like you're ill."

"How dare you!" Abby shouted, her face turning red.

Noble got right in her face. "How dare *me?* You bring your sympathetic sorry self to *MY* country, and pretend like you care about us, about me, when really you could care less —"

Abby became bolder than she ever had been in her life. She grabbed Noble's face and silenced him with a kiss. Her lips were burning hot like the wood in a fireplace in the middle of winter. He tried not to respond to her prodding lips, but she palmed the back of his head and pulled him in as close as she could. His anger rushed to his groin in a current of hot perplexity, causing him to moan.

Their lips wrestled while their eager tongues dirty danced. Lips and tongues threw violent jabs at one another as if they were in a prizefight for the Heavyweight title. Noble came to his senses and his eyes flew open as he shoved her away. He wiped his mouth with the back of his hand like he just tasted something vile. Abby's chest rose and fell as she gasped for breath.

"Did *THAT* feel like a person who doesn't care about you?"

Noble snorted again. "Typical American woman. You think throwing yourself at me is going to change something? I know your kind. I just regret believing you were different. Silly me. I should have never trusted you! Well, your conscience can rest easily now, you've done your good deed for the year. Now go back to where you came from. I don't ever want to see you again! You got that?" Noble turned on his heels and stormed off, leaving Abby convulsing in a current of bitter tears and wounded sobs.

****

Her name was Selena. A slender, svelte, half-Jamaican, half-Haitian immigrant, from nearby Carrefour. Her jet-black skin always shone with golden glitter or platinum flakes from body make-up. Selena was a 24-year-old rebellious woman with lots of face piercings and tattoos. Her twisted sense of reality, and pleasure for pain, made her the perfect counterpart for Slice and Bête Noire.

Slice had seen her several times before the earthquake in dive-bars and local hangouts, but he kept his distance because she wasn't really his type. Plus, she preferred women over men for the most part, so he paid her no mind. It wasn't until one of his trusted men suggested he meet the sadistic woman with the gold tooth that Slice agreed to a face to face.

Selena walked into Slice's office wearing short shorts and a fishnet tank top. She looked around and nodded approvingly at the tastefully decorated space. Heavy artillery and leather all around announced it was a thug's lair of ample proportions.

Slice reclined in his swivel chair with his massive size 14 Air Jordan's perched up on the mahogany desk. He puffed on a blunt while she entered. He did not stand up to greet her. Instead, he nodded towards the chair in front of the desk. Selena took her seat. When she smiled, Slice stared at her 24k gold tooth. The diamond S engraved in it sparkled brightly.

"My guys said you're a tough one. Got three, four, bodies under you belt, and that you get off on torture," Slice said. He looked at her facial piercings in bewilderment.

"*Six* bodies to be exact," Selena corrected him proudly. "And I wouldn't really call it torture. I just get off on pain. Giving *and* receiving it," she said seductively.

Slice grunted and blew smoke in her direction. "Do you smoke?" he asked.

"I'm part Jamaican, what do you think?"

Slice leaned across the desk and passed her the blunt. Selena's long, four-inch nails grasped it and she took leisurely pulls from the potent cigar like a pro.

"Do you know what type of operation I'm running?" he asked her.

"Not really," she shrugged and blew three perfect rings of smoke towards the ceiling. "But I heard rumors. They say you're taking over the country and trying to rule with an iron fist. Get down or lay down is the motto we've been hearing over in Carrefour."

"Yeah, that's it alright. Haiti has been soft for far too long. It took the earthquake for me to realize we need someone who can run things with force around here!" Slice connected his fist into his palm for emphasis. "Power. That is what every man wants. Without it, he is nothing. Nada. These Teddy bears I pulled the rug out from under had no heart, no guts. They didn't deserve their positions. So I took it," he said and laughed harshly. Selena passed him the half-smoked blunt back. Slice took a few more drags before continuing.

"Bête Noire means to be viewed with fear. As long as the people are afraid, they will obey. I'm making the frightened join my regime and help rebuild *MY* country the way that I want it built. Things are coming along as planned. The millions of dollars coming in from all over the world goes directly into my hands."

"Oh yeah? How'd you manage that Slice?" Selena inquired.

"Extortion, ultimatums, you know, the usual no holds barred tactics involving force and seizure. Either way, I have say over every dollar donated to poor old Haiti. Once my empire is built, we'll see what's left over for the people. If they're lucky, the money will continue pouring in and we can put up a few schools and clinics again. If not?" he shrugged and extinguished the blunt in a marbled ashtray.

"Sounds like a good plan. And from what I can see," Selena paused to look around at the gold fixtures and expensive décor. "It's working quite well for you. But it's one thing you were wrong about Slice."

"Hmpf. Oh yeah? What's that?"

"You said power is what every *man* wants. Well, I'm *all* woman, and I too share in your ambition for dominance and power."

Slice looked at the Hershey Kisses push through the mesh material. *She's clearly excited*, he thought to himself and licked his lips. "Hmmmm, is that so?" he breathed heavily.

"Mhm," she said, rising to her feet slowly. Slice snapped his fingers twice and the handful of machine gun toting men who were in his office exited immediately.

Once the two were alone, Selena walked around and sat on top of the desk. She put her feet on the arms of Slice's chair and rested on her elbows. The smile on her face said it all.

"Bête Noire is about to make history baby. You wanna be a part of it?"

"I would love to," Selena responded enthusiastically.

Slice stood up and unbuckled his belt. "Well… show me."

Chapter 14

When The Seeds Grow

By the time Noble realized his construction endeavors were not for the restructuring of Haiti, but rather for the benefit of Slice, it was too late. He had been manipulated and played like a puppet. The whole time Slice fed Noble a cockamamie story about wanting to change his image in the eyes of those who feared and disliked him. In reality, his plans grew more devious and wicked by the day. Slice used his relation to the prime minister —a distant cousin of his — as bait.

He told Noble he was requested to partake in government restructuring and needed his expertise in architectural design and construction. They were going to build a new and improved Haiti that would be unbreakable.

Noble was never a dumb man, but the sudden resurgence of his love life had turned him uncharacteristically naïve. Love had a way of doing that to a person. It wasn't until the young man Ares confronted Noble that the light finally dawned on him.

"Noble, at first I thought you had your own agenda going on by following Slice's plans," Ares said.

It was a cool afternoon. They leaned against the new gymnasium Noble and his men were putting the finishing touches on.

"What are you talking about Ares?"

"You really don't get it do you?" Ares said and shook his head. "All of the donations, all the money... everything goes to Slice. You think the National Palace is still for the President's administration? That's Bête Noire headquarters!"

"What?"

"Happy Abby's really blinded you hasn't she Nobe? You're as green as a pool table, and twice as felt," Ares remarked.

"Ares, you're still a teenager. You couldn't possibly know nor understand what's going on. *This*," Noble opened his arms and did a 360 turn, "is all for the new and improved Haiti."

"No. *This*... is for the evil greed of Slice and his gang."

"If his gang is so evil, and his plans are so devious, then why are you a part of it?"

"That's the million-dollar question isn't it?" Ares smiled at him. "Walk with me for a sec Nobe. You knew my parents pretty well, right?"

"Your mother and Genevieve were good friends. I knew *of* your father, but he sort of went by his own rules," Noble said, referring to the outspoken, ex-military man that created Ares.

"Yeah, pops was a bit of a hothead. People have said if he had been an American, he surely would've been a Black Panther. That's where I got my revolutionary spirit from. Him and 'Pac." Ares referred to the late-great rapper Tupac Shakur. Someone his father listened to on a daily basis.

"You see this?" Ares pulled his glistening YGM pendant from under his shirt. "Young Goon Militia. That's *my* clique. The ones I ride and die for. Screw Bête Noire!" he shouted, waving his middle finger in the air. "We infiltrated that clown's regime so we could see how we could take him down from the inside."

"Ha! Now you think you're an undercover officer or something?" Noble taunted.

"No, I'm not undercover anything. I'm a proud Haitian that refuses to let him destroy what's left of our country."

Noble put a hand on Ares' shoulder. "So, none of the money coming in is going to the Haitian firms and organizations?"

The fact of the matter was corruption ran rampant in places of power. Of the $9 Billion that came from foreign governments, multilateral institutions, and private donors, only 6% of that money found its way to the government. USAID (United States Agency for International Development) dispersed 2.13 Billion dollars, but only 48.6 million (2%) of that went where it was supposed to go.

"None of it. Where do you think all the branches of government are? They are either dead, blackmailed, or extorted, by you know who."

"What?" Noble exclaimed.

"Yeah. Rumor has it he kidnapped some key members and is holding them for ransom until he gets what he wants. I don't know exactly *who*, but his men get loose at the mouth when they're drunk, so they let things slip out."

"That sounds ludicrous!"

"I know, but it's true. Préval is only alive for show. He is easily controlled and afraid of Slice. Once he serves his purpose… " Ares ran his thumb across his throat.

"And his administration?"

"The ones that didn't comply bit the bullet."

"Did you get involved Ares?"

"Me? No. We don't harm innocent people, but I have stood by hopelessly and watched Bête Noire do some pretty terrible things that made my blood boil. I couldn't do anything though. I have to make them believe I am *with* them, and when the time comes… " Ares shrugged and trailed off.

"If what you're telling me is true, what can you possibly do to Slice? Don't take this personally, but you're still a kid."

"Well Nobe, I **am** taking that personally. And fine, underestimate me if you want to. Underestimating is a weakness in the eyes of a hunter, but it's the strength in the mind of the prey. Remember that. There can only be one winner, so the opposition who miscalculates his opponent becomes the vulnerable one." Ares stated.

In that moment, Noble no longer looked at Ares as some teenage boy, but as a man who picked up some great wisdom in his young life.

"Do you know the origin of my name Noble? My parents named me after the son of Zeus. That larger than life Greek figure that was the God of War. They knew I would one day become a dominant, radical figure that would put Haiti on his back and carry us into the future."

"You're very ambitious. I didn't know you were sooo… "

"Smart? Wise?" Ares laughed. "I know I'm young, but I've been on my grown man stuff for a while now. Playing chess has taught me how to be a thinker. How to calculate my moves steps ahead and prepare for the worst. I've learned a lot of Slice's ins and outs behind the scenes. Things like how he's seized the Post Offices in order to collect all the donation checks and financial aid coming in via mail. Hundreds of thousands of dollars from all around the world!"

"*That's* why I didn't get her letters," Noble said.

"Huh?"

"Um, nothing. Go on."

"Well, he gets a kick out of our Young Goon antics when we get rowdy. This lets his guards down and gives us easier access to the information we need. Slice has it in his distorted mind that he's gonna conquer the whole world somehow. The money he's accumulating right now offers him a certain amount of power. He wants to be more feared than Papa Doc."

Noble gasped, François "Papa Doc" Duvalier was Haiti's most vicious ruler that birthed the most brutal paramilitary organization in the hemisphere. If Slice went that route, it would be extremely bad.

Ares continued. "Lil' Bête, as he calls us young ones, are poised to become the foot soldiers of the regime. Mostly, he uses us as decoys, saying we're displaced refugees."

"How is he planning on running the government? He knows nothing about politics."

"We all know that. But he's doing more than dabbling in politics. He's had meetings with Cartel members from South America, Mexico, and Nicaragua. Slice is investing a lot of money into drugs, weapons, and human trafficking. He plans on turning Haiti into the worlds #1 tourist attraction. Lavish resorts, Casinos, and all the vices a foreigner can handle, will be at their disposal. It's not going to happen though. There are more of us youth, than it is of them. We're young goons on the outside, but trained militants on the inside," Ares said, tapping his temple with his pointer finger.

Noblesse looked at the young man. All five feet and 100 pounds soaking wet of him. His baggy blue jeans and over-sized T-shirt made him look like any kid in a rap video. His fitted baseball cap sat on top of a bandana wrapped around his head. The AK-47 strapped to his back was practically bigger than him, yet he handled the assault rifle with ease.

Reading Noble's mind, Ares said, "Do you remember Xavier's Dad? He was our military's arm specialist when we were pups. From the time Xavier knew how to walk, his dad was teaching him about weapons, shooting, and various strategies in war. Before he died in Tropical Jeanne, Xavier was already aligned to be his father's predecessor. FRAPH (The Front for the Advancement and Progress of Haiti) took Xavier to various countries for the Summer and trained him in everything from sharp shooting, to bomb building, and disabling them. His knowledge on espionage is ridiculous. How do you think I know all of this? Kids are into that kind of exciting stuff. We soaked it up like a sponge. I'm telling you Noble, Xavier has more connections than the UN! Through X, we have a contact system and never-ending supply of weapons that Slice knows nothing about. One by one, we're going to quietly knock off his regime so that Haiti can be restored to justice and placed in the hands of *GOOD* people."

"Like you?" Noble questioned.

"Or someone like *you.* After all, I'm just a teenager, right?" Ares said smiling.

"I don't think Presidency or great power suits me well. That's a lot of responsibility. I like to work with my hands. Politics require the kind of brain mechanics I don't have, but it sounds like you do," Noble admitted honestly.

"Thanks man. You're one of the greatest leaders I've ever met. And you're a people person that comes from a historic bloodline." Ares referred to Nobles great ancestor François Toussaint L' Ouverture. The former slave who led a successful slavery revolt that helped Haiti become the first Latin American country to achieve its independence in 1804.

"Either way, whoever it is, it sure won't be Slice. *That,* I can promise you," Ares said.

Noble nodded his head slowly, digesting the information Ares laid on him. He was baffled at how that could go on under his nose. Was he really *that* blinded by love?

"We all knew this day would come Noble. My father knew. Xavier's father knew. We've been training for years. When you come from a country ran by dictators for hundreds of years, you are taught to accept a certain way of life. Not us. We may look young, but we're not dumb. It's a great disguise for the unsuspecting though. *Aww, poor snotty-nosed hip-hop kids with no homes. They don't know any better.* That's how people look at us. If they only knew… "

They looked at the sky. Noble said a silent prayer to the man above. Rays of sun flickered across his face as the clouds played peek-a-boo in the sky.

"You're serious huh?"

"As a heart attack. Look, Noble. You've got a good woman by your side. Happy Abby is super cool, a little square, but she's good people. Take her back home and *stay* there. Start from scratch. Make a new beginning in the States. They say it's the land of the free. You don't want to be around here anymore. Things are about to get *really* ugly."

Noble shivered. "How do I know what you're telling me is the truth? This could be some decoy you're making up so you can knock off Slice and continue doing what he's doing, but on a grander scale. After all, you do call yourselves *GOON* militia."

"You're right. You don't know if I'm telling the truth. You'll just have to take my word for it… or not," Ares shrugged.

"Do you remember when I was like eight or nine? Me and Ricardo got caught stealing candy bars from Mr. Duconts' store. You gave us the money to buy snacks, but we pocketed the money. When you asked us why we did it, we said we lost the money. You knew we weren't telling the truth. You sat us down and said, *never look an honorable man in the face and lie to him. The dishonesty in your heart will corrupt your soul. When you steal from those who work hard with their hands, you assassinate their ethics and heap shame upon your family's name.*"

"At the time, we didn't want to hear a lecture on right and wrong, but the seeds you planted grew into positive lessons that remained with me for all of these years. In a way, your advice and philosophies shaped me into the person I am today.

Yeah, I may look like a young street punk, but I'm street smart *and* book smart."

"I can see that. I didn't know how intelligent you were, Ares," Noble said, quite impressed.

"I love to read and learn new things. I was told from a young age that I would need knowledge and wisdom to succeed in life. So I soak up everything I can. Good or bad. Sweet or sour. Whatever it is, I apply it to my life in the best way that I can. Noble, I'm looking an honorable man in the eye right now. I'm telling you. I am no decoy. Nothing fake or phony is in my blood. This is 100% genuine Ares Ali Andoux, speaking from the heart. My soul is far from corrupt, and I have a duty to protect my country and leave behind a legacy like your ancestors did. It's what I was born to do. It's my purpose."

Noble looked at the young man with respect and adoration. To know one's calling and accept it as Ares did was admirable. "Hmm, ok. But what's with this *GOON* business?"

Ares laughed. "Oh, yeah, it's not sweet. "We're some beasts alright, but not *evil* ones. We fight for a good cause. Goon is an acronym. It means **G**ood **O**pposes and **O**verrides **N**egativity. A Goon is also someone who does away with their opposition, if one opposes a good way of life, we do away with them. Plus, it sounds soooo gangsta! It has a ring to it. I love it! YGM will ride or die for the cause. It's no secret that kids need to feel a part of something in order to fully function. That's why so many lost souls get into the kinds of trouble that they do. Well, even though I'm wise beyond my years, I am still one of *them*. I want to show my peers a better way of life. The whole world needs help, man. It's gonna take more than one person though. I want kids to see we can all be leaders."

"Now you sound like a preacher," Noble joked.

"I've been told that from time to time. I'm not really a religious dude, but I believe in God. I know He's up there watching over us. I'm far from an Angel. I'm ready to put those demons wandering the earth to rest," he said, patting his gun.

"Get your girl and go back to the States with her. I'll send word to you when things have calmed down." Ares suggested.

Noble thought about the major projects put on hold. Slice said they couldn't work on places like the Children's Hospital, the High School, and Holy Trinity, until the country received more funding. All lies. Noble burned with anger and an emotion he wasn't accustomed to; *hate*.

He looked at the young man. Ares looked like your average teenager at first glance, but on the inside, he possessed the mind of a scholar, the heart of a champion, and the soul of a warrior. *If this is Haiti's future, we're in rather good hands,* Noble thought to himself. All his mentoring and positive reinforcements to the youth obviously paid off because Ares made Noble extremely proud at that very moment.

"Alright, Ares. I'll do it, but how will I leave without Slice getting suspicious?"

"I was hoping you'd ask that. Here's the plan... "

Chapter 15

It Is What It Is

It was Noble's first time in the Presidential Palace since its reconstruction. He redesigned the skeleton of what it *used* to be and added a new flair of resilience to the legendary structure. Slice however, dressed it like a royal thug's palace. It was still under construction, so Slice took up the west wing of the Palace because it suffered the least damage.

Noble's team of construction workers welded beams and poured concrete around the clock on the property. He addressed his men with "good job" and "looks great, keep it up," as he observed their blood, sweat and tears in action.

The earthquake made the second-floor collapse in an awkward way. The attic floor lay in heaps of rubble around the columned central pavilion, while places like the kitchen, and historical library, were barely touched.

Thou which reads, gains seeds. Growth is what supersedes. Where one feeds, give thanks to holy seeds, do good deeds, and you will eat like Kings.

Noble and Abby were ushered into the dining area by "Elephant," aka Phant, Slice's right-hand man. There was a never-ending table that sat 100 guests.

Now that Ares removed the wool from over his eyes, Noble could see where all the money from the empathetic souls was *really* going.

In the center of the table was a Dom Pérignon fountain. The bubbly champagne overflowed a one-hundred champagne flute pyramid. One-hundred Backwoods were scattered across the elaborate tablecloth.

Butlers brought in trays of King Crab, jumbo shrimp, steak, lobster, lamb, various pastas and side dishes. A roasted pig sat on a silver platter, covered in a honey glaze, with an apple in its mouth. Wine, beer, Hennessy, lean, and Crown Royal were the other beverages being consumed in abundance. There was a dessert table against the wall with forty different tasty concoctions on it.

Slice, who normally donned jeans or cargo fatigues, was wearing a three-piece tailored suit. His wing tip oxfords shone like gold bars. Bête Noire cleaned up well too, wearing their Sundays best for the evening.

Noble and Abby were escorted to the massive table. Slice gave them a courtesy nod as they sat down. Key political figures Noble thought were legit, sat toward the head of the table by Slice. Smoke permeated the air in clouds, from the many cigars being smoked. Abby coughed and fanned her face which got a bout of laughter from the regime.

"Can't stand the heat, you better get out of the kitchen!" Selena said to Abby and laughed shrewdly. Noble and Abby had never seen the scary looking woman before. She was chugging from a half empty Hennessy bottle as she stared them down. Her purple eyeshadow made her dark skin look menacing. Abby shivered. Selena gave her the heebie-jeebies.

Slice stood up and raised a glass in the air. "To the nouveau riche!"

"Nouveau riche!" Everyone repeated and clinked glasses as they toasted to "the newly rich." Slice walked the table putting his hand on the shoulder of his guests. He thanked them for their contributions to the reconstruction of Haiti. The Prime minister, head of CARICOM, members of International Fund for Agriculture Development, CEO of World Bank Group, Minustah from the peacekeeping UN branch, several divisions of government, and social councils, were amongst the attendees drinking champagne like it was water. A blind man could see the this was a table of rich and powerful individuals. And Slice had them all wrapped around his finger.

"I will now show you what the *NEW* Haiti is going to look like," Slice announced and waved his hand. The heavy double oak doors opened, and Slice's men wheeled in a 3D model display that looked like the Caribbean version of Las Vegas. 10 floor resorts, and massive hotels, surrounded lavish Casinos, Nightclubs, and Shopping Malls.

There were Condominiums over-looking the ocean, Luxury car lots, Strip clubs, and Plazas with fluorescent Massage Parlors and custom jewelry stores.

Everyone ooh'd and ahh'd as they gasped at the beautifully constructed visual. Slice pointed to the different attractions, and the revenue each place would bring.

Noble sat in complete shock. There were none of the schools, churches, or community centers they had discussed.

A middle-aged woman from UNICEF asked about the education and medical facilities.

"*This*," Slice motioned to the conceptual model, "is just a visual perception of the things we'll build around the education and medical facilities. There was no need to put those in the model because they will automatically be restored in their previous spot. In a better condition of course. These are just bells and whistles to get our country out of poverty by attracting tourists," Slice lied.

Noble was not buying it. He knew Haiti like the back of his hand. The places where those "automatic" schools and facilities were supposed to go were substituted in the model by some grand business scheme or resort of some kind. There was no possible way to include any of those facilities because of the gargantuan structures cluttering the city.

"Our great friend, Noblesse here," Slice announced as he walked behind Noble's chair and put a hand on his shoulder. "Is head architect and engineer responsible for turning this model into a real-life experience for us all."

Noble grimaced. It was obvious Slice was playing the attendees in the room as well. He went from a complete thug, to a polite and literate instructor, at the snap of a finger. A real two-faced devil in the flesh. Everyone applauded and smiled in Noble's direction.

"Noble is a great man, hence his name. He has vowed to see this thing through until Haiti is fully restored and resurrected 100 times greater than it once was."

People nodded solemnly and Slice continued to pour it on thick. He called on the heads of the organizations in attendance. Telling them they would be relied on to pool their resources and contribute in whatever economical, medical, and agricultural fields they were in.

"The sooner, the better. Even as I speak, our people are still digging bodies out of the rubble. Remains that have been buried for weeks. Kids are still wandering the streets looking for their parents, and vice versa," Slice shook his head.

"It's sad. I want to do all that I can for those people. I was lucky, as were all of you. We survived. Many did not. So, give generously. We need your help." Slice finished his spiel and received a standing ovation while he took his seat at the head of the table.

Selena stood beside him and clapped proudly. She smiled and her gold tooth sparkled under the chandeliers. Something about that woman made Abby's skin crawl. She told Noble she had to use the restroom and made a quick break for the exit. Slice saw Abby get up and he nudged Selena in her direction. As soon as one of the servers occupied Noble with an entrée, Selena slipped from the room like a ghost in the night.

Abby was literally sick to her stomach. The doctor told her severe nausea could be a side effect from the chemotherapy treatments, but she wasn't sure if it was from the chemo, or the despicable display of BS from that con artist Slice. Either way, she heaved her guts out as she clutched the solid gold toilet.

A few minutes later, she exited the stall feeling lighter and somewhat better. Abby turned on the cold water in the sink and rinsed her mouth out several times. She held her head in the sink, admiring the marble detail as she cupped water in her hands and sipped from them. She closed her eyes and splashed water on her face.

When she was done, she decided to take some selfies in the immaculate bathroom. She got so lost in her picture taking, she didn't hear anyone enter.

"Oh my God!" Abby exclaimed when she saw Selena in the mirror. She was behind her, leaning against a bathroom stall.

"I um… I didn't hear you come in. You startled me," Abby said and sat her phone on the sink.

"They never do," Selena said with a wicked smile on her face. When she strode toward Abby, her stilettos clicked on the marble floor while she spoke.

"Sooooo, you're Noble's new flame huh? I've seen you around, helping out here and there. A regular ol' do good ameri*CAN* ain't cha?!" Selena got in Abby's face and laughed crudely. Then, she hissed, and she sniffed Abby's neck like a dog. Abby tensed up and stepped backwards.

"Fear is a scent that is a turn-on for the hunter. I can *smell* how scared you are, little miss helper. Mmhm. It's doing something to me." Selena whispered in Abby's ear. She tried to make a run for it, but Selena grabbed her by the ponytail and yanked her head back.

"Listen here. You're going to leave Noble alone so that he can build our empire, and you're gonna make sure that he does it too, or his only child will be no more," Selena hissed and wrapped an arm around Abby's throat. With her free hand, Selena held a cellphone in front of them and played a video. A young girl was chained to a chair in an empty bedroom.

"But… " Abby gasped, Noble's whole family died in the earthquake, she was puzzled.

"Slice found her in a cabinet. A miracle she was still breathing. He knew little Queen Jean would come in handy when it was time to *persuade* Noble."

Abby couldn't believe it. Angry tears spilled from her eyes. The pain in her heart for Noble squeezed harder than the woman did around her neck.

"That's impossible. Noble would have found his daughter. He's combed this entire island," Abby wheezed.

"You must remember, Noble was in the hospital for a while when the earthquake hit. Slice seized the opportunity immediately, and began his takeover," Selena laughed shrewdly.

Abby stared at the deranged woman in the mirror. Her gold tooth sparkled when she laughed. If what she said was true, Jeanette-Mary would have been held captive for months.

What have they done to her in that time? Abby thought to herself. The girl in the video looked terrified. A dirty bandana was tied around her mouth as tears stained her baby face.

"If you promise not to hurt the girl, I will do whatever you want," Abby conceded.

Selena howled and cackled to the marbled ceilings. "We thought you'd see it our way." Selena ran her long fingernails down the middle of Abby's shirt slowly. The smile on her face caused Abby to flee the restroom immediately.

Her heart was beating rapidly as she ran into the dimly lit hallway. She could hear Selena's evil laugh behind her. She looked to see if the woman was in pursuit, but no one was behind her. She was so focused on what was behind her, that she didn't see the four giant men in front of her. Abby ran head-first into one of the big men and fell flat on her butt. The men laughed as she shook off the stars and birds circling her dizzy head.

"You should watch where you're going little miss helper," Selena said. Her high heels click clacked down the corridor while the men helped Abby to her feet. Abby looked around dazed and terrified. They had her surrounded. She looked up at the men who were taller than Noble. "I... I... "

"You, what?" Selena said as she approached. Her body glitter and facial piercings shimmered like moonlighting on a lake. The hallway was so dark, all Abby could see were the gold lips and white teeth of Selena as she spoke. "You can donate money to our cause if you wish, but I'm giving you 48 hours to get out of Haiti... or else!"

"What about Noble's daughter?"

"We will reunite her with him once he completes our project. Until then, she will remain in our custody."

"How could you do such a thing? She's just a child!"

One of the men grabbed Abby's arms and held her hands behind her back. Selena circled Abby as she spoke. "Hey, this isn't personal... it's business."

"Abby! Are you out here?" Noble called out.

"Shhhh." Selena pressed her pointer finger against Abby's trembling lips. "Remember what I said..."

The man let her arms go and Abby took off running. Noble was standing at the end of the hallway. When she reached him, she leapt into his arms and tried to hold back tears.

"Are you ok? What's wrong?" Noble asked. He hugged her tightly and looked over her shoulders. He could hear laughter and high heels clicking down the hallway, but he couldn't see anyone in the darkness.

"Noble, let's get out of here, please," Abby begged.

He didn't need to be told twice. Noble built the place, so he knew every exit on the compound. They snuck out without anyone knowing. Before they drove off, Abby dropped the bombshell in his lap. Nobles only response was a lone tear that slid down his cheek. He gripped the steering wheel until his knuckles cracked. He looked at Abby and vowed to get his baby girl back.

"I know Noble. And I will help you find her. I'm with you."

Chapter 16

The Rescue

Dr. Moore had a beautiful mansion that sat on the Caribbean Sea. It was a ten-thousand square foot estate that Noble designed and built ten years prior. Not only was Dr. Moore critical in saving Noble's life, he was also the same Dr. that brought his three miracles into the world.

"Happy birthday Doc. You really went all out on this affair," Noble commented.

"Thanks Noble. With everything that has gone on this year, I wanted to throw a celebration that people could enjoy."

Noble looked around at the decorations and themed activities going on. "Who wouldn't enjoy these festivities?"

"Well, my friend. Walk around and enjoy yourself. We'll share a toast later," the Doctor said.

"Will do," Noble said, and walked off to find Ares.

He took deep breaths to calm himself and silently prayed for strength. As much as he was seething inside, he had to keep it together if he was going to fulfill his mission.

When Noble entered the kitchen, he found Ares sampling the food and cracking jokes.

"Oh, Ares, you are so adorable," a conservative woman in a little black dress commented. She pinched his cheeks and smiled. Ares was entertaining Daniel and Susan Avigdor — a wealthy investment couple — when Noble walked up to them.

"Noble! Hi there, buddy. How's it going?" Daniel greeted him with a hearty pat on the back.

"Blessed," Noble replied.

"Sooo, Noble," Susan slithered in and grabbed Noble's arm. "When is the resort project going to be done? That *does* have first priority, right?"

"Now, now, Suzie Q. Don't go pressuring the man," Daniel said as he extracted his wife's hand from Noble's bicep. "I'm sorry about that Noble. She's just excited to see our dream–"

"Hey, it's fine. Look, I need to speak with Ares for a minute. We can chat about the project later," Noble told them. They nodded and walked away.

"How'd it go?" Ares asked.

"I didn't punch the guy, so I'd say it went pretty good."

"I admire your self-discipline. If it was me? I would've snapped! Dr. Moore is a snake—"

"Ares. He will get what's coming to him. For now, we must get my baby girl," Noble reminded him.

"You're right. I will keep an eye on things while you get her. Make sure your earpiece is in. I'll let you know if someone's coming," Ares said.

Noble put the tiny Bluetooth in his ear and nodded. "Ok. I'll let you know when I have her."

"Alright. Be safe, and good luck."

When the coast was clear, Noble walked to the back of the kitchen. A maid came down the spiral staircase and nodded at him. He returned the favor and headed upstairs. His destination was the Library.

****

"They are hiding her at Dr. Moore's mansion." Ares said to Noble. They were at Kiara's house where Jeanette-Mary's whereabouts were being revealed.

"What?" Noble exclaimed.

"Abby was recording selfies when Selena cornered her in the bathroom. Their whole exchange went on long enough for my tech guy to do his detective work. We got Abby's phone and pinged the location of the video she saw. It came back to an address in Jérémie," Ares said.

Noble recalled the dream home he designed and built for the doctor ten years prior. It was a beautifully constructed 10,000-square foot estate that overlooked the Caribbean Sea in Jérémie, Haiti.

"Noble, I want a room that no one knows about. My own little hidden haven I can escape to and do whatever I please." Dr. Moore revealed to Noble during the construction of his

dream home. Noble built that "getaway haven" for Dr. Moore. It was a hidden mancave behind a bookcase in the library.

"I don't get it though. Why would she be there? Dr. Moore would never —"

"Noble, he's in on it," Kiara said.

When Abby told Noble about the video of the girl, he didn't want to believe it was his daughter. He asked Ares to find out about any girls being held against their will, and that uncovered another ugly side to Slice and his activities. The worst part of it all, trusted members of the community like Dr. Moore had their "Mr. Hyde" sides.

Once it was confirmed that Jeanette-Mary was alive, they constructed a plan to save her and flea to the U.S. right away. Abby had a friend from the missing and exploited children organization who owned a plane. That G6 would idle on the Grande Cayemite island and take off as soon as they boarded.

Abby was told she'd be needed to drive the getaway boat to get them out of Jérémie and get them to Grande Cayemite. She was terrified, but she was all in.

****

My own little hidden haven I can escape to and do whatever I please. Those words replayed over and over in Noble's mind while he made his way down the hall. He hoped his hands didn't create the hell cell that caused his daughters' pain.

When he got to the Library, he froze. He did not want to know about the evils that went on behind that door. He pondered the worst possibilities as he turned the doorknob.

"I'm in. Is everything clear down there?" Noble said into his earpiece.

"Yeah, you're good." Ares responded.

Noble walked to the bookshelf and grabbed the green leather Bible. The thick book was actually a lever that opened the bookcase.

Noble opened it just enough to get in. He felt the wall for a light switch while his eyes adjusted to the dark. When his finger pushed a button that shed light on the room, it also caused him to shed a pool of tears.

His daughter was curled up in the fetal position, peacefully sleeping on a bare mattress.

"Queen Jean. It's me baby. Daddy's here," he said as he knelt beside her.

The girl's eyes got big when she saw it was her father. Tears and snot mingled while she sobbed in his arms. Noble removed the bandana tied around her mouth and wiped her face with it. He rocked her in his arms and consoled her.

"Noble. He's headed upstairs. Do you have her yet?" Ares chirped in.

"It's gonna be alright, baby girl. I'm here. I'll never let anyone hurt you, ever again." Noble assured his daughter.

"Oh Daddy. I'm so glad to see you," Jeanette-Mary wept. I thought I'd never see you again. Dr. Moore said —"

"Shhh. Don't worry about that honey. Let's get you out of here," Noble said, and picked her up.

When he pushed the bookcase open, Dr. Moore was entering the Library. They locked eyes for an eternity.

"I can't let you take her out of here, Noble."

"How could you? I trusted you," Noble shook his head in disgust.

"It's my flesh. It's weak. It's dirty. So, so, very dirty. Do you remember when I said your leadership and integrity is the only thing that can fight the perils of evil? Well, I was referring to *me*. You are the purest man that I know. If this world is going to have any chance at survival, we need more Noble's. In a few years, *she* will be able to create them for us."

They both looked at the girl cradled in Noble's arms. A lone tear rolled down his face as he faced his demons. "If you want me to spare your life, I suggest you get out of my way," Noble said as he walked toward the door.

"Noble, I can't let you —"

Ares opened the door and pointed a gun at Dr. Moore. "Go Noble. I'll take care of him. Just get out of here."

Noble did as Ares said. On the way out, he broke the doctor's nose with one punch.

Ares held the doctor at gunpoint while Noble and Jeanette-Mary escaped through a window. The several mile hike down the embankment was tiring and messy because the grass was slick with dew. They fell and slid most of the way, but eventually they got to the bottom.

When Abby saw them, she cranked the 1800 horsepower on the Magnum Express cruiser. Jets of water shot from beneath the speedboat while Noble and Jeanette-Mary boarded.

"Queen Jean, this is Abby. Abby, this... this, is my daughter, Jeanette-Mary," Noble choked up while he made the introductions.

Abby looked back and smiled. "Nice to meet you Queen Jean. Ya ready to get out of here?"

"Yes, please." Jeanette-Mary replied.

Abby looked straight ahead and sped off. There would be no looking back for the three of them.

PART THREE

New Beginnings

Chapter 17

Queens First Christmas

"Whatchu want done?"

"Excuse me?" Jeanette-Mary responded.

"Done? How, you, want, nails, done? You like French tiiip, Gel, glossy?" the foreign nail tech asked.

"Giiirl, little miss thing here is a Queen, into the bling," Jenny interjected and laughed.

"Ohhh, bling bling. Ha, ha. Well, let me know design, and I do. Now come. Put your foot here." The nail tech patted the foot bench.

Jeanette-Mary didn't understand the language the lady was speaking. She looked at the exchange between Jenny and the Asian woman. Their smiles and laughter were organic exchanges of communication. The vibes were good, so she did as she was told.

"Ahhhh, that's good," Jeanette-Mary moaned. Abby and Jenny giggled. It was Queen Jeans first Christmas in America.

Abby wanted to take her somewhere fun, so they took a girl's trip to the Mall of America. Before they shopped, they got mani/pedis.

Twelve luxury Pedicure Spa Chairs occupied the back room. Jeanette-Mary melted when her feet touched the hot water. The Whirlpool shot jet blasts of a bubbly concoction that would leave her feet rose petal soft.

"So, how's it feel?" Jenny leaned over Abby and asked.

"Are you kidding me? This is ohhh... "

"Well, you still need to pick your nail design," Jenny reminded her.

Jeanette-Mary had tuned her out by then. Her head was deep in the leathery cushions as she closed her eyes and relaxed. Her nine-year-old feet had been through a lot in life. *Too* much. It was time to wash away the journey they trudged.

When she wanted to end it all, a light at the end of the tunnel peaked through and gave her new life. She felt the pain and pressure of her journey wash away while she listened to the banter of the other customers.

"In ten years, this city will burn like never before," a lady said. The room suddenly grew silent.

"The drink that you despise, will be the virus that kills you in the year of perfect eyes, if you don't avoid your favorite food's countryside."

"Chiiiild, I don't know *what* chu talking 'bout," a woman with six-inch nails said. "But umm, you killin' our vibes up in here lady. You can —"

"Killing *your* vibes? Hmpf! Because of one killing ten minutes from this very mall, in ten tears years, the tears will burn tall."

"Listen, I don't even know what you're saying. You are making absolutely *no* sense. But your nails are on fleek though," she laughed and flipped her wrist.

"Whoooa, those are cool," Jeanette-Mary exclaimed. "I want something like that!" She grabbed the woman's hand who sat next to her. Two fingernails on each hand were adorned with Crystal diamond gems.

"Now, now Queen Jean. It's rude to grab other people's hand like that," Abby said.

The young girl released the woman's hand and hung her head. "I'm sorry. I just —"

"Hey, it's ok. You like my nails huh?"

There were a dozen women sitting in the Whirlpool Spa Pedicure Chairs. Jeanette-Mary was mesmerized by the woman who frantically waved her hands. She and a woman in all-red, went back and forth about something. It was live entertainment for her. She couldn't resist her bouts of laughter during their exchange.

"You like these, little mama?" the woman asked Jeanette-Mary.

"I doooooo," she said with bug-eyes.

"Ha!" The woman in red barked. She looked at Abby and said, "When you say those two words, the boogeyman will appear on your most anticipated day."

"Ma'am, what are you trying to say?" Abby asked.

The woman didn't respond. She just looked around the salon and pointed to the women.

"You've *all* been warned. Remember that. You were told things that will impact your life in one way or another. Take heed… or else."

"Or else, what?" A beautiful Chilean woman said. "I just got my husband back. He was buried alive for 69 days! We came here to celebrate life, and I have to hear *this?*" She shook her long black hair.

"Oh my God! What happened?" Abby asked.

"My husband of eight years was in a mine in Chile, when things went terribly wrong. He and thirty-two others were trapped underground for sixty-nine days. By the grace of God, he was unharmed when they rescued them," the woman kissed the rosary around her neck and made the sign of the cross.

"My God, that must've been terrifying for you," Abby said.

"It was. Faith and prayer got me through it. And look, it worked! I have my husband back, and we're trying to have a baby," she gushed. Everyone in the salon congratulated her.

After their pedicures were done, Jeanette-Mary knew how she wanted her nails done.

"Can I get something like hers? But maybe with a crown instead," she pointed to the animated woman with the gems on her fingertips.

Abby and Jenny nodded their heads and smiled. They were glad Jeanette-Mary was able to enjoy the moment. The young girl had watched her entire family die and was then abducted for months. Her well-being was holding up fairly well under the circumstances.

"You sure can Queen Jean. You can get whatever you want," Jenny assured her.

When they returned home, she couldn't wait to show her dad her nails and all the gifts Abby and Jenny bought her.

"Ooh, those are pretty," Noble told his daughter. "Look at you. I'm going to have start calling you Queen Bling," he joked. They all laughed. "So, how was your trip to the mall?"

"Oh dad, it was great! They have a Lego store, a build your own teddy bear store... even a rollercoaster inside!"

"Whaaaat? They do not," Noble responded.

"They do to. And look. They even had a cool candy store," Jeanette-Mary rifled through her shopping bags and pulled out a giant Gummi Bear.

"Wow!" Noble smiled.

"I know, right? I can't wait to go back. Abby and Jenny said we can go again for my birthday. Will you come with us dad?"

"Of course, I will sweetheart."

"Hopefully that creepy lady in red won't be there again."

Noble's eyes bulged. "Lady in red? What lady in red?"

"Oh, just some drunk woman rambling on about a bunch of nonsense. It was nothing really," Abby interjected.

Noble grabbed Abby's shoulders. "What drunk woman? What did she look like? What did she say?"

"Calm down, Noble. It was just some young chick talking hogwash," Abby assured him.

"Yeah, dad. She was weird and all, but it's nothing to get worked up about," Jeanette-Mary told him.

Noble looked from his daughter to Abby. He did not want to scare them, but he had to find out about the lady in red.

"About how old was this woman?" he asked.

"Late-twenties, early thirties at the most," Abby responded.

"Did she have dreadlocks?"

"No. She wore her hair in a short ponytail. Why all the questions Noble? Do you know her or something?"

"No. Not at all. I'm just trying to grasp a better concept of this weird human being you two speak of."

Abby kissed Noble on the forehead. "Nothing to grasp honey. It was just nail salon banter."

Noble watched Abby walk upstairs. An uneasy feeling in the pit of his stomach told him it was more than nail salon banter.

Chapter 18

Starting From Scratch

A young woman in a pink dress walked up to the podium. She looked at the hundreds of faces staring at her. "Good evening. My name is Renee. I am a two-time survivor." Everyone in the room stood up and clapped. The standing ovation of support brought tears of joy to Renee's eyes. A few women on the stage threw a consoling arm around her.

"I'm here for a purpose. Cancer showed up at my doorstep, and I fought it... twice! There was a point when I was on my death bed, but by the grace of God, I'm alive and cancer-free today." The room erupted in another round of applause that led to another standing ovation.

"Before I introduce the next speaker. I would like to Thank my good friends Noble and Abby for helping me get through this battle. The humanitarianism and love that you two show," Renee sniffled as she began to cry. "It's truly amazing. Your organization not only helps people start new lives from scratch, but it plants the seeds needed for a better future. Thank you so much for all the help and support. I'm forever in your debt. I love you."

The crowd gave Noble and Abby a round of applause. They stood up and acknowledged the love.

"Our next guest is a writer and poet from Milwaukee, Wisconsin. Ladies and gentlemen, please give him a hand," Renee said as she passed the microphone to an impeccably dressed man. Once the applause died down, he spoke.

"The first time we met, I did all of the talking. It was refreshing to have someone finally *listen* to me. She was unique in her form, thin and colorfully vibrant. One day she was blue, the next she was black, I never knew what color she would show up in.

As the years passed by, she never changed. I on the other hand, *did.* She helped me transition into a man from a kid. Growth and development led to deep mental elevation. She was my teacher, helping to mold each creation. A versatile personality with vast views so eclectic. Oh my, what an imagination my first love has.

As the world morphed into the digital age, she began to disappear for weeks at a time. She said she was busy, yet I'd see pictures of her on social media, having the time of her life… with others.

I'll admit. I denied her quality time. My own life was a roller-coaster ride of highs and lows that I had to manage. Through it all, I always held a special place in my heart for her.

There is nothing like her. A unique immortal, that expresses herself freely. Her true self isn't impersonal, although people try to make her that way. I scoop her up into my loving arms and hold her tenderly as I say…

I will always love and cherish you, for the man you have helped me to be. They may not appreciate you, but you are forever in my heart, eternally.

Your art is slowly dying, your colorful tears are drying, baby I'm so sorry. If I have to resuscitate you, I will keep your heart beating. Your pulse will forever throb, as long as I am breathing.

When I kiss her with my fingertips, the results are oh so exciting. In case you didn't know... my first love, is writing!" He smiled and received a round of applause.

"Writing is my therapy. It is the passion that gets me through the trials and tribulations life throws my way. Dozens of women in my family either battled or died from Breast Cancer." People in the room gasped and nodded knowingly. "I use my art and passion not only for release, but also to teach. To motivate and inspire someone holding on to their last shred of sanity. If you have something to contribute, please do." The man stepped back and exited the stage to more applause.

Noble gave his testimony and explained why his organization SFS was an important one. "We are two people who lost everything and built this from the ground up. Our only mission is to help whoever needs restoration."

"Excuse me, may I speak with you for a second?" Abby stopped the writer as he exited the stage.

"Oh, hi there. Sure, what's up?"

"Well, first I wanted to thank you for that beautiful piece you shared," Abby complimented him.

"Why, thank you. I wrote it specifically for this event."

"Oh, gosh. Gee, thanks Duane. That's pretty awesome."

"Yeah, so what's on your mind?"

"Well, I know you write everything from poetry to music, but have you ever considered writing books?" Abby asked.

Duane laughed. "Well, I've actually written a few of those too. Nothing you would've heard about, but yeah, I've dipped my toe in the novel game before."

"Oh, ok. Well, that's even better then," Abby stated.

"Why is that?"

"Because I want you to write me and Noble's story."

"Umm, I don't know if I'm the guy for that. You guys have that fairy tale story that would be good for Nicholas Sparks."

"Duane, we don't know Nicholas Sparks. But we do know *you*. Well, kinda," she laughed. "Look. You have the kind of raw talent that would enhance our story and help bring awareness to several causes. You said your purpose is to motivate and inspire right? What better way to do it than to share what we've been through? Trust me Duane, it is *far* from a fairy tale."

Duane pondered Abby's proposal when he saw Noble walking up behind Abby. Duane took a couple steps backwards.

Abby wondered if her laughter was off putting, or maybe her breath was not so good if the young writer visibly moved away from her.

When Abby turned around, Noble was on one knee. He took her left hand in his and smiled.

"There was a point when I had nothing to live for. When you lose everything in the blink of an eye, it's hard to foresee any kind of a future. But even in my darkest hour, God brought me a guardian Angel by the name of Abby."

There wasn't a dry eye in the room as Noble poured out his heart. Abby held a trembling hand to her mouth as tears ran down her fingers.

"Abby. We have been on a journey from the day we met. We've battled diseases, lived through natural disasters, and escaped the Grim Reaper more times than I can count. You have been my ride or die companion from day one. Let's continue this new life as Mr. and Mrs.… Abigail Winters, will you make me the happiest man in the world, and marry me?"

"Yes! Yes! Of course, I will!" Abby shouted as she jumped up and down excitedly. The room erupted in loud applause and celebratory congratulations.

"Does this mean I get to come to the wedding?" Duane stepped forward and asked.

Everyone laughed and hugged.

Chapter 19

Fairytales & Nightmares

The sun was shining brightly. The forecast predicted a rain-free day. That was great news for the guests sitting outdoors. Noble and Abby held their memorable "I do's," at an outdoor ceremony, by the lake.

The wedding aisle was a six-foot wide, twenty yards walk of pink and white rose petals. People chatted, ate, drank, and tapped their feet to the smooth grooves the DJ played, before the nuptials.

Beautifully arranged bouquets — in the shape of hearts and cancer ribbons — were displayed on chairs, tripods, vases, down the aisles, and perched on the alter and pulpit as well.

When Abby walked down the aisle, she looked and felt like every woman wanted to feel on their wedding day. She radiated beauty and love. Her heart was whole, and her soul was nourished. It would be a day to remember.

Abby's uncle Pat walked her to the altar. She asked if he would give her away, and he gladly accepted.

Abby smiled at the guests on both sides as she gingerly walked on the rose petals. Her train dragged as *Here, comes the bride*, played softly.

She couldn't wait until the four-minute walk was over. *Thank you, God*. She mouthed to the willows hanging from the sky.

The bridesmaids and groomsmen all had a pink hue on their tasteful attire. The men wore pink shirts or bowties, while the women wore floor-length pink and white chiffon gowns.

There was a beautiful array of roses that covered every square inch of the property. Noble and Abby's wedding was a survivor themed celebration that displayed positivity and good vibes all around.

When Abby got to the altar, Pat shook Noble's hand and congratulated him. When Pat walked off, Noble took Abby's hands in his.

"You gave me hope when I had none left. You mended my broken heart and showed me how to love again. You helped bring my daughter back to me and gave us a new life. Now I will spend the rest of mine, making you the happiest woman in the world, Happy Abby."

"Thank you so much," Abby sniffled. "Noble. You are the bravest, smartest, most compassionate man I have ever known. You have been by my side through my most difficult times, and you were patient with me when I know I wasn't the easiest person to get along with. I love you with all my heart and soul. I will honor you for the rest of my life."

The priest laid a hand on each of their shoulders. "Noble. Do you take Abby as your lawful wife, to have and to hold, from this day forward, for better or for worse, for richer or for poorer, in sickness and in health, to love and cherish, until death do you part?"

Noble looked at his best man Ares who smiled and nodded. Noble squeezed Abby's hands and penetrated her eyes with a loving gaze. "I do."

"Abby. Do you take Noble as your lawful husband, to have and to hold, from this day forward, for better or for worse, for richer or for poorer, in sickness and in health, to love and cherish, until death do you part?"

Abby cheesed from ear to ear. "I do."

Ares gave Noble a ring and he slid it on Abby's finger. Jeanette-Mary then gave Abby a ring that was blessed by the priest before giving it back to her.

"I take this ring, as a sign of my love and faithfulness," Abby said and slid it onto Noble's ring finger.

The priest nodded and continued. "These two are about to become a true union of God. If anyone here objects to this marriage, speak now, or forever hold your peace."

"I have something to say!" A voice rang out.

An audible gasp went through the crowd as everyone turned around in their seats. The sinister voice came from a man in a tan hoodie and khakis. He walked down the aisle with a cocky strut as he spoke. "I object to this union. It isn't *official*, until the person who brought these two together, is here."

Ares and Noble exchanged alarmed glances but kept their cool. The man walked up to the pulpit and paused. He placed a hand on Ares' shoulder and whispered. "You did good, but not good enough."

He then stood on the altar between Abby and Noble and rested his forearms on each of their shoulders. "Since you guys always have a shoulder for people to lean on," Slice joked. "Look. *I'm* here now, and I give you two my blessing."

The priest was shocked by the grisly man's interruption. He didn't want any more disruptions, so he got straight to it.

"Noble, do you?"

"I do."

"Abby, do you?" The priest asked.

"Yes, God, I do!" Abby exclaimed.

"By the power vested in me, I now pronounce you man and wife." The whole church erupted in applause and whistles. "Noble, you may now kiss your bride," the priest said.

Noble looked at Slice and gave him a look that made him step down. Slice obliged and stood next to Ares.

Noble lifted Abby's lace veil. He knew the sudden bomb in the middle of their nuptials would rattle her. Her pretty hazels

were alert with danger. "Pie face, baby. I've got this. Hey…
look at me," Noble told her.

Abby's eyes focused on her man. His handsome face and
sincere voice penetrated her soul. "Kiss me like you'll never
see me again," Noble instructed.

Abby palmed the back of Noble's head and brought her lips
to his. The hoots and hollers helped seal the moment. Noble
lifted Abby up and spun her around and around while they lip
locked through all their emotions.

Tears mingled. Smiles were mirrored. They laughed and
silently spoke plans to each other, all during their epic kiss. By
the time he put her down, Abby was Mrs. L' Ouverture, and
planning an escape route from the boogeyman.

A girl can't catch a break, Abby thought to herself. She put
on an iron-clad smile that lit up the room. She poked her chest
out and lifted the bouquet as high as she could. All the women
screamed and rushed to the altar.

Abby spun around and faced the priest. She counted to three
and threw the bouquet over her head. Eager hands clawed for

it, while women screamed and battled for a wish. There was a light tug of war between two women who did not want to relent, but the woman shouting for joy and holding the bouquet high, was the obvious winner.

"Yeah! I got it. It's gonna be *my* turn now," the pink haired woman exclaimed.

****

"Job well done Noble," Slice said as he clapped slowly. "You managed to escape my grasp and start a new life here in the States. I bet you thought you'd never see me again, huh? Well, you were wrong. I'm baaaaaack."

"Slice, why are you here? Why would you come and ruin my wedding day? Can't you just leave us alone?"

"Noble. Because of you, I lost everything. I had it all —"

"*You,* lost it all?" Noble snapped. "Slice, you stole from people. You corrupted top officials and took innocent lives. You deserved to go to jail."

Slice laughed in his face. "You're funny Noble. *I* deserve to be caged like an animal? Nah, man. Not me. Can't no prison bars contain me. When you have the power and influence that I have, there are ways to get what you want. In this case, I wanted my freedom. I wouldn't miss your wedding day for all the money in the world," Slice smiled and patted Noble on the shoulder.

He cringed and shrugged the evil man's hand away. "Slice. You have already caused a scene and disrupted my ceremony. You've upset my wife and daughter. Now would you please leave?"

"Not before I congratulate the Mrs." Slice attempted to head in Abby's direction, but Noble blocked him.

"You will do no such thing. Leave. Now!" Noble demanded.

"Jeez Nobe. You're awfully rude. I've traveled an awfully long way, and I'm hungry. The food looks delicious. Do you mind?"

Noble looked around. A lot of eyes were on him and Slice. He didn't want bad vibes in the air, so he relented. "Help yourself, and then do me a favor and please leave."

"Ok, ok. I know when I'm not wanted," Slice threw his hands in the air and walked toward the buffet.

Noble's daughter rushed to his side. "Dad. What's he —"

"Queen, don't you worry about him honey. I'll handle this. Go and join your mother," Noble instructed.

"Yes, Dad," the teenager replied.

Noble huddled up with his groomsmen. He eyed Slice from a distance while he and the guys went over a quick plan. When everyone knew their roles, they all dispersed.

"Hi, beautiful. May I have this dance?" Noble asked his blushing bride who was surrounded by enthusiastic women.

"Why yesssss. You sure may," Abby responded with her deep southern drawl and signature smile.

Noble took her in his arms and pulled her close. He could feel her rapid heart beating against his own chest. "I love you, pie face."

"I love you more, my handsome man," Abby said and caressed his face.

"Don't let him ruin our day. I promise, I'll take care of him."

"Just be careful sweetheart," Abby said and kissed him.

"I will."

Chapter 20

Garbage Disposal

"Slice, you're on your third plate," Noble commented as he stood next to his enemy.

"I told ya. I came a long way. I'm hungry, man." Slice said and piled food on a dinner plate.

"Alright. Well, try some of this." Noble added some gumbo to the several other entrees on his plate. "We need to talk though. Come with me." Noble gestured to the terraced gardens behind the buffet.

Slice licked his fingers and lifted his shirt. Noble saw the .45 in his waistline and shrugged. "Just don't get any ideas," Slice warned.

Noble nodded and took the first steps. Slice stuffed his face while they walked under orange and lemon trees that swayed.

"Nice décor ya got here," Slice mumbled.

Noble cringed. He couldn't enjoy the prettification put in by his daughter and wife. Their hard work and preparation had been overshadowed by a black cloud. A fungus. A plague.

"Thank you." Noble replied.

"And this food... man... " Slice spoke between bites. "This is... mmm... this is the best catering —"

"It isn't catered. My wife cooked it. *All.*" Noble said proudly.

"Mmm, really? Didn't know she could cook like that.

"How would you?"

Slice shrugged and shoveled more food into his mouth. "Either way. This is good eating. They don't feed you that well in prison, ya know?" Slice licked his lips and sucked on a chicken bone.

"I wouldn't know about that. I live the kind of life that keeps me away from places like those," Noble responded.

"Ahh, ever the upstanding nobleman. Well, not everyone is as *righteous* as you are Noble. Some of us were dealt bad hands and —"

"Spare me the bad hand, poor me, excuse Slice. I know plenty of people who had harsh upbringings. That didn't turn them into psychotic killers though."

"Ouch. You really know how to cut deep, don't cha Nobe? Hey, I could have come after you when you left. But I didn't. I let you be. Even though my empire did not get built, and I went to jail. I still forgive you."

"Forgive me?! You abducted my daughter and held her —"

"Ah, ah, ahhh. Dr. *Moore* held her hostage," Slice corrected him. "Either way, what's done is done. You have a new life, a new bride… life's good. Isn't it Nobe?"

Noble looked out into the valley. One thousand acres of vineyards shone in the afternoon sun. Noble waited until Slice finished his plate before he spoke.

"Slice. Life is good. Do you see that beautiful ocean?" Noble pointed to the body of water in front of them.

Slice began sweating and coughing.

"That is the same ocean I crossed to get away from you. I thought I'd never see you again."

Slice coughed and grabbed his neck. He began to wheeze.

"What's wrong Slice? Cat got your tongue?"

Slice staggered to the pavilion where he could sit down. "H-H-Help... me," he pleaded in a light whisper.

Suddenly, Ares and half a dozen men entered the pavilion and stood behind Noble.

"I may have been wrong about seeing you again, but I will never make that same mistake. Ya know Slice, the funny thing about my wife's cooking... she uses peanut products in almost *everything*." Noble said and smiled.

Slice's eyeballs bulged out of his head at the mention of peanuts. He began to gag and tried to make himself throw up. Slice fell to the ground and tried to reach for his gun, but Ares disarmed him. Slice's respiratory and cardiovascular systems shut down as he foamed at the mouth and convulsed. Noble walked off to join his new bride in holy matrimony and did not look back. An hour later, Ares joined him at the reception.

"Noble, the trash has been disposed of. Your burdens have been castaway."

Chapter 21

Catch-22

Several modeling agencies saw Queen Jean's Instagram posts and took a unique interest in her. There were a few places she wanted to audition at in person, so her family took her to Italy for her twenty-second birthday.

To be in the fashion capital of the world was a dream come true for Jeanette-Mary. Her biggest passion was modeling and being in the heart of it made her one step closer to her dream.

They spent the first couple of days taking her to appointments and shuttling her around the city.

Late afternoons were "family time," where they toured the town and did fun activities like Gondola rides, hikes in the mountains, and wine tasting tours.

On the evening of their private boat tour, they had dinner at a beautiful restaurant that sat on the Adriatic Sea. Abby, Noble, and Jeanette-Mary dined on Maldon-salted sirloin, with julienned vegetables, paccheri pasta, and warm cheese fondue. They conversed about the baby names and everyone had their own opinions.

"If it's a boy *and* a girl, name them King and Queen," Jeanette-Mary said with a smile.

Abby rolled her eyes. "Of course, you would pick those names, wouldn't you? Well. I would love a Noble junior. Honey, what do you think? And if it's a girl, maybe Genevieve?"

Noble looked at his daughter. They smiled at each other and nodded. "I love it. I don't know about the junior, but if it's one girl out of those two, I was definitely thinking Genevieve," Noble replied.

"I don't know dad. I kinda like the junior idea. It has a nice ring to it. I didn't think of that one. Now that you mention it mom… mom? Are you ok?"

"Huh? Yeah, I'm fine. Why?" Abby asked.

"Your nose is bleeding honey," Noble said and used his napkin to dab her nose.

"Oh, my. I-I-I'm sorry," Abby said and held her head down.

"Don't apologize pie face. It's not your fault. Are you ok?"

Abby held the cloth to her nose and looked up at her family. She didn't want to tell them she felt extremely dizzy and sick to her stomach. It was those parts of pregnancy that she wasn't looking forward to. "Yeah. Let me go clean up in the restroom. I'll be back," Abby excused herself from the table.

"Dad. Mom didn't look so well."

"I know honey. It's probably just her pregnancy symptoms."

"Yeah, dad, you're probably right." Jeanette-Mary played with her hair. "Wow. I can't believe it. I'm gonna be a big sister!"

Noble admired the genuine smile on his daughter's face. He finished his beer and sat the bottle on the table. "It's a blessing from God. I... I can't believe it either."

"Believe, what?" Abby interjected as she sat down. She smiled and looked like her normal self again.

Their waiter appeared. "Would you like another beer, sir?"

"Um, yes please."

The waiter retrieved Noble's empty Corona bottle and asked if he could get the ladies anything.

"No, we're fine," Jeanette-Mary answered.

When the waiter left, the three of them joined hands and prayed. "Heavenly Father, thank you for this meal before us." Noble bowed his head and spoke. "As we gather to celebrate our daughter's birthday, we would like to thank you for the two bundles of joy growing inside of Abby. May they grow up to be strong, holy people that do the right thing and show love and compassion to all of mankind."

"Dear Father God, thank you for all of the blessings you have poured upon us. Thank you for loving us even when we don't deserve it. Please unite the families that have been separated. Give strength to the weak and feeble. Keep watch over your people and send them guardian Angels in their time of need. In Jesus name I pray," Abby said.

"Amen." The three of them said in unison.

****

After supper, they went for a walk. The Renaissance architecture really captured Noble's interest. The Cathedrals, Artisan shops, and classic sculptures throughout the city, became the backdrops to their family photos.

By the time they got to Piazza della Signoria, Abby was short of breath and wheezing. "I think… I need, to, sit down."

Noble and Jeanette-Mary sat Abby under a peculiar statue and fanned her.

"Here. Drink some water," Jeanette-Mary instructed. She held a bottle of water to Abby's lips. After a few sips, Abby spit the water out and coughed.

Noble patted her on the back. "You're not looking so hot. Maybe we should head back to the hotel."

He felt Abby's forehead. "Oh my God! You're burning up!"

Jeanette-Mary put the back of her hand to her mother's forehead. "Whoa, you're right dad. Maybe we should get her to a hospital."

"No, no, no! There will be no hospitals on our vacation. I'm just a little hot is all. I'll be —" Abby stood up and fainted.

When she came to, she was in a hospital room. Her family, a doctor, and two nurses stood at her bedside.

"Mrs. L' Ouverture. How are you feeling?" Dr. De Rossi asked.

"Uhh… tired." Abby looked at her daughter and husband. They were wearing face masks. "What happened? Why do you guys have those things on?"

"You fainted honey," Noble said and squeezed her hand.

"Mrs. —"

"Please. Call me Abby."

"Yes, of course. Abby, you have contracted COVID-19. It's also known as the Coronavirus." Dr. De Rossi stated.

"Huh? Coronavirus? I don't even drink beer. *He's* the Corona lover," Abby pointed at Noble.

The doctor laughed lightly. "No, Abby. This is an airborne disease. Kind of like the flu, or the common cold. That's why we have these masks on. It's highly contagious."

"So, I have the flu? Great."

"I'm afraid this is a bit more serious than the flu. Because of your previous health conditions, you have low eosinophil. That is a specialized immune cell needed to fight this virus."

"Doc, I've beat Cancer *twice*, and survived a few natural disasters. Just give me what I need to kick this virus' butt!"

"As much as I would like to do that, there is no cure for this… this, this, *thing* yet. It's fairly new and has been affecting people at an alarming rate."

"Oh. So, what are you saying?" Abby began to worry.

"We will keep you hydrated with fluids and morphine. We are going to watch you overnight. If your symptoms diminish, we will discharge you. But for now, rest and hydration are the best remedies," the doctor said and patted her knee.

"Nurse's… let's leave them be," he said and left the room.

Abby sighed loudly. "Thanks a lot, Noble."

"For what?"

"Giving me some virus with your stupid Coronas!"

"Honey, it's not that kind of Corona," Noble retorted.

Abby smiled weakly. "I know. I'm just fooling witcha. Boy oh boy. If it's not one thing, it's another."

"Mom, we'll get through this. Whatever it is. You've got this beat!" Queen Jean assured her.

"Noble, will you turn on the TV, for me love?"

"Sure, sweetheart." Noble grabbed the remote and did as his wife asked. Everyone in the room wish he hadn't.

"Health officials have ordered anyone who has come into direct contact with a person who's tested positive for the Coronavirus, to be quarantined for 14 days."

"Quarantined? What's that supposed to mean?" Jeanette-Mary questioned the newscaster.

"I don't know, but it sounds serious," Noble replied. They spent a couple of hours watching the news. It didn't take long for Queen Jean to fall asleep in her chair. Noble draped a blanket over her and sat next to his wife. He pulled the face mask down and smiled. "I love you pie face. To the moon and back," he caressed her face.

"I love you more," she replied with an adoring smile.

Chapter 22

Going Home

"I get it now," Abby laughed and coughed.

"Get what?" Noble questioned. It was late and they were reminiscing on all the good times.

"Everything she said. It wasn't mumbo jumbo at all. Do you remember when Jenny and I took Queen Jean to the mall?"

"Which time?"

Avoid your favorite food's countryside...

"When I met the miner's wife."

"Oh yeah. At that Mall of the World," Noble said.

"Mall of America," Abby corrected him and laughed. That caused a bout of coughing that went on while she spoke. As much as she loved to laugh, doing so racked her chest in painful spasms that took her breath away.

"There was a woman... " Abby coughed.

"Take it easy, sweetheart. Relax," Noble stroked her hair.

"This woman in red —"

Noble bolted upright. "What woman in red?

The drink that you despise…

"What's my favorite food?"

"Pizza. Why?" Noble asked.

"What do I always harp on you for drinking?"

"Coronas?"

"Yeah. She told me… she told me…"

Will be the virus that kills you in the year of perfect eyes.

"What? What did she say?" Noble demanded.

Abby sobbed. "I-I'm sorry, my handsome King. I didn't listen to her. I —"

"Queen Jean mentioned her that night. I remember now. You said it was a drunk woman talking nonsense. It was her, wasn't it? Wasn't it?"

Abby nodded her head while tears rolled down her cheeks. Noble leaned over the bed and kissed them off her face.

"You were persistent in knowing more about her. I thought it was because she was young and pretty —"

Noble placed a hand under Abby's chin. " I didn't know what the woman looked like. And even if I did. I have eyes for only *you*. Pie face, you should know that."

Abby sniffled. "I know. I wish I would've —"

"What's done is done. We cannot wish for what's in our rearview. All we can do is look forward and enjoy the scenery ahead of us. Abby, just like you told the doctor... you've battled cancer and natural disasters, you surely can beat this."

Abby smiled weakly and squeezed Noble's hand. They both stared at the moon and thought about their couple's motto. *Love you to the moon and back.*

"Noble. You know I love you, right?"

"Of course, I do. I love you too honey."

Abby began to cry. "I can't wait to see you change diapers and bounce our miracles on your knee. You're already a great father. Our kids are in good hands."

"Yeah, but they're coming into a messed-up world that isn't so kind to certain people." Noble commented.

Abby knew he was referring to inner-racial humans that endured harsh and real-life consequences because of their skin. She looked out the window and stared at the moon. Her love for Noble extended as far as the natural satellite shining down on them.

Abby bowed her head and closed her eyes to pray.

Noble followed suit and held her hand in silence. Once his pleas and feelings were cast to the man above, he said. "This year hasn't started off so good honey, but I promise you, when we get through this, things will get better."

He thought about the *It gets greater, later*, motto he adapted.

Noble spoke encouraging words that offered hope and inspiration to a despondent situation. He poured his heart out.

After a while, when Abby didn't respond, he looked over and saw that she fell asleep. Noble pulled a blanket up to her chin and kissed her forehead.

He walked to the window and looked at the stars. He knew in his heart of hearts that there was something bigger than he could ever grasp, up there. He said a silent prayer.

"Please Lord. Have mercy on my family. I try to live a righteous life and give back as best I can. I'm not perfect, and I hope you can forgive me for my transgressions and backslides. God, please don't take her away from me... "

When Noble woke the next morning, the sky was gray and dreary. Raindrops beat against the windowpane angrily.

His daughter was still curled up in her chair, snoring lightly. When he looked at Abby, his lips trembled. Her eyes were closed, and her skin was blue.

Noble stood over her and kissed her ice-cold lips. His tears covered her face while he hugged her tightly.

"Noooooooooo!" His roar was a lament that ripped through his heart. The 7.0 he survived was nothing compared to the magnitude his soul felt.

Author's Notes

There are people who were forced to start from scratch because they lost their jobs. When the Coronavirus struck, the whole world shut down. Everything from factories, to mom and pop shops, were closed by the government.

Even the very place everyone went to drown their sorrows at were mandatorily shut down. That didn't stop some bars from trying to get their money. Having customers come through the back, kept their stacks intact.

Hurricane Katrina claimed 1,800 lives in 2005. Five years later, Haiti's 7.0 claimed hundreds of thousands of lives. That same year, 33 miners were buried alive for 69 days. They were rescued and lived to tell a story of hope.

New decades symbolize new beginnings. For many of us, that is all we want... A fresh start. Out with the old, and in with the new, as we transition into something we hope for.

2020 started off somberly with the death of an icon and a pandemic that no one saw coming. The Coronavirus has killed more than 650,000 people worldwide.

280,000 women and 2,600 men are diagnosed with breast cancer every year. Those numbers do not factor in the numerous other types of cancers that affect people annually.

When these catastrophic spectacles impact our lives, all we can do is battle them with faith and courage. Prayer, positivity, and perseverance are the three P's needed to combat our problems.

Real-life isn't always pretty. We long for the fairytale-ending but end up experiencing things we did not wish for. When this occurs, you must remain optimistic and hold your head high. No matter how bad you think you have it, there are people around the world going through much worse.

Count your blessings and be thankful for what you have. Put good energy into the universe and watch it reciprocate.